Garrett stared at his son's photo.

Anjelica kept her gaze on Garrett's face as he stared at the top photo of t̶ Not able to resist, she pe̶ d saw a seriou̶ en-gray eyes sta̶

Garrett p̶ yes.

Moving ba̶ ̶ed to give him space to collect him̶ A broken heart was nothing new to her, but to watch such a controlled man fighting to hold it together made her want to wrap him in her arms.

He handed her the photo, paper-clipped to an information sheet. "I don't know how to do this, being a father."

"We can make it work." She blurted it out. Thinking of what had happened to those two small children, she knew they needed a home full of love and good memories. Tears started burning her eyes. "We have to make this right for them. We have to bring them to a real home."

He looked at her. "We?"

A seventh-generation Texan, **Jolene Navarro** fills her life with family, faith and life's beautiful messiness. She knows that as much as the world changes, people stay the same. Vow-keepers and heartbreakers. Jolene married a vow-keeper who shows her holding hands never gets old. When not writing, Jolene teaches art to inner-city teens and hangs out with her own four almost-grown kids. Find Jolene on Facebook or her blog, jolenenavarrowriter.com.

Books by Jolene Navarro

Love Inspired

The Soldier's Surprise Family

Jolene Navarro

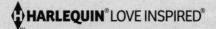

HARLEQUIN® LOVE INSPIRED®

Recycling programs
for this product may
not exist in your area.

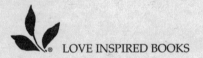

LOVE INSPIRED BOOKS

ISBN-13: 978-0-373-71979-2

The Soldier's Surprise Family

Copyright © 2016 by Jolene Navarro

www.Harlequin.com

Printed in U.S.A.

Consider now, for the Lord has chosen you
to build a house for the sanctuary;
be courageous and act.
—*1 Chronicles* 28:10

This story is dedicated to the military families
that support, serve and protect our nation.
Especially Baron Von Guinther for talking
with me until the wee hours of the morning in
San Diego, brainstorming this story and
helping me get to know the hero, Garrett Kincaid.

Chapter One

Texas state trooper Garrett Kincaid scanned the yard, hoping to find it empty. The afternoon sun had gone into hiding as the breeze carried the aroma from the overabundance of flowering plants. When he arrived home from a long shift, sleep was the only action item on his agenda. Ha, he was funny.

His garage apartment offered sweet seclusion a few steps away. He might actually avoid a conversation or another offer of a meal from his energetic landlady, Anjelica Ortega-Garza. She threatened his resolve to stay out of relationships. There was too much to like about her. He even liked the way she said her name with the Spanish pronunciation. It rolled off his tongue so smooth. He shook his head and made himself stop playing with her name. It was just a name.

It took so much effort to tell her no. He had to admit he'd never eaten so well. According to his mother, pushing buttons on a microwave counted as a home-cooked meal. And during their short marriage, Viviana's favorite dinner came in a to-go bag.

Another scent mixed with the flowers and he knew coffee and bacon were close. The lady could cook. She seemed to have an overdeveloped need to feed the entire population of Real County and every resident within a hundred-mile radius.

"Stop right there. Don't even think about it!"

Firm and sharp, the command stopped Garrett mid-motion. He turned to find the lady who had just been in his thoughts. Standing with her hands planted on her hips. Petite and lovely, she looked in charge. A purple scarf got caught up in the wind before she tucked it back into place.

He groaned. His resolve not to think of her in a personal way took a hit every time he saw her. So much for avoiding her.

Her normally friendly smile was gone, replaced with a glare, but not at him. A few feet away from her, a silky mop of a dog lay on its belly. Big brown eyes darted between Anjelica and a small herd of colorful chickens. Maybe they were a flock. *What do you call a group of chickens?*

He'd grown up in the city surrounded by noise, not hills and odd farm animals. A month ago he would have told anyone who asked that he was a city boy. But living fifteen miles from a town that was in the middle of nowhere, Texas, he discovered a new side of himself. And a new plan, to build a home of his own where people wouldn't bother him, especially an overly friendly landlady.

The one-room cabin would sit on the edge of the Frio River. He could see the waters running so clear it washed all the grime away from life.

He sighed. After his disastrous marriage, the biggest part of his plan was to stay single, no ties and no family. There was a sign over Anjelica that screamed Hero Needed and he vowed to never play that game again.

A small whine sounded from the silky mop with a pink bow. Maybe he could still make it up the stairs to the apartment over her garage. He glanced to the door, estimating how long it would take to—

"Officer Kincaid!"

He dropped his head before turning to face her. The woman made him nervous with her whimsical smile and dancing movements. Fragile and naive, someone else who needed to be protected from the real world.

Her golden-brown eyes found him, bright and eager. The commander of a moment ago vanished as she made her way toward him. The fluff of a dog that Garrett had never seen before followed, deciding to chase her flowing skirts instead of the chickens. "How was work? I always pray nothing happens." Her eyes slipped to the gun he had holstered at his hip. "Uneventful night in your line of work is a good thing, right?"

"Yes, ma'am."

"I saved a couple of extra soft tacos. Egg and bacon along with fresh coffee. I can bring them to you."

"I—" Before he could find a good excuse, Sheriff Torres's patrol vehicle pulled into the drive and parked behind his SUV. An unexpected visit from the local sheriff usually brought bad news.

Anjelica's smile vanished. She clutched her scarf with one hand as the other held her stomach. She displayed all the signs of someone who knew to expect bad news. In a few steps he closed the gap between them.

A woman in a fitted business suit and low heels got out of the passenger side. She was tall, with her dark blond hair forming a neat bun. In his cowboy hat, Sheriff Torres approached with the woman close behind.

"Morning, Anjelica. Kincaid." He nodded to each of them and shook their hands.

Garrett watched as Anjelica took a deep breath, in and out.

"Kincaid, this is Sharon Gibson. She's with CPS."

Child Protective Services. Relief loosened the muscles he hadn't even noticed had tightened. So it was work related and they were here for him, not her. He gave Anjelica a reassuring smile. Her shoulders dropped a notch and her smile returned. She moved to the woman and shook her hand.

The woman turned to him, offering a greeting. In her free hand, she carried a couple of folders. "Nice to meet you, Officer Kincaid."

"Likewise. So, what can I do for you?" The one thing he dreaded the most was domestic situations involving kids. He turned to Torres. The sheriff shook his head. Garrett's brows crunched inward. Now he was confused.

Sharon Gibson cleared her throat. "We're here because of your son in Kerrville."

"Excuse me?" There was no way he'd heard that right. He glanced at the sheriff's grim face. "I don't have any children. I've never even lived in Kerrville."

"You were married to Viviana Barrera Kincaid while in Houston, correct?"

"For a short time."

She tilted her head. "Are you saying her son is not yours or that you are unaware of the boy, Garrett River Kincaid Jr.?"

The world stopped spinning. Where had his blood gone? Glancing down, he noted that his body looked intact. Muscles pricked as if drained.

The woman looked around. "Is there somewhere we can sit and talk?"

His mind had gone blank. Sit? She wanted somewhere to sit? Behind an invisible wall, he watched Anjelica pick up her dog. Words were exchanged.

She walked to her porch and disappeared into the house. The woman, Sharon Gibson with CPS, followed her onto the porch and sat on a rocking chair.

Commands from his brain went unheard by his body. Nothing worked. Frozen. Viviana had found a way to pull him into her drama all over again.

Torres stopped next to him, placing a firm hand on his upper arm. "I take it you didn't know about the boy. No one likes being blindsided." The sheriff patted Garrett's tense shoulder. "Come on—we'll get this worked out."

A son, no way. There had to be a mistake. Viviana, for all her faults, would have told him about a child. It had to be Ed's, her boyfriend she kept going back to. How could they know for sure that the boy was his? He was going to be sick. Deep breaths.

He followed Torres up the steps, not seeing anything but the folders on the low table between the chairs.

Anjelica pushed open the screen door. The hinges needed to be oiled. She sat a tray on the small table. "I have sugar and cream. Does anyone need something else, like water?"

Sharon smiled. "This is perfect, thank you." She poured cream into her cup.

Garrett stared at the swirls of the white getting lost in the black liquid.

"Garrett?" Anjelica's voice brought him back to the present. The warmth and smile were gone. Now he got the same glare the chicken-chasing dog earned. He was a dog.

He shook his head. If he tried to drink or eat anything, it wouldn't stay down.

At the end of the porch, across from Sharon, Sheriff Torres sat on the swing and took a drink from his cup. "Sure you don't want coffee? Maybe some water?"

"I'll get you some water." Anjelica disappeared into the house.

Sharon took a sip before she looked at him, a soft smile on her face. "So you were married to Viviana Barrera?"

Breathe, Garrett. You have to breathe. He nodded. His throat too dry to make a coherent sound.

"Her son's name is Garrett River Kincaid Jr. You're listed as the father on his birth certificate. Family members also say you're the father."

"Are you sure?" What kind of man didn't know he had a kid? Even his loser of a father stuck around for the first few years. "I didn't know." His jaw hurt, but he made sure to keep his face calm. A clear mind and facts, that was what he needed to sort this out.

"This is an emergency situation. You can challenge with a DNA test if you want to, but the state uses the name on the birth certificate and acknowledges you as the legal father."

Garrett looked at the curve of the rocker resting on the worn boards of the porch. What had Viviana done now? He cleared his throat, the need to explain, to make them understand, burning his gut.

He heard the creak of the screen door again and looked up. Anjelica handed him a water bottle. Fighting the urge to press the cold bottle against his neck, he rolled it between his palms. His landlady vanished inside the house again. "Why are you the one telling me this? Are they in trouble?" If CPS was involved, something had to be wrong.

Sheriff Torres leaned his elbows on his knees and

Sharon took a deep breath. He wanted to yell at them to stop messing with him, but he sat and waited. He pressed his right thumb into the center of his left palm. He could hear the chickens in the yard and music playing somewhere in the house. None of it seemed real.

"There's a history of domestic violence with her current boyfriend."

Viviana's life was a history of domestic violence, from the time she was born. The need to save her had eaten him for years.

"Yesterday a neighbor called to report shouting and gunshots. Two bodies were found. It looks as if he shot her, then turned the gun on himself. It's under investigation. The officers found the boy, Garrett, his baby sister and a dog hiding in the backyard."

All the blood left his body. If Sharon kept talking, he didn't hear it. Viviana was dead. Grief and regret swamped him. She was dead and she had left children behind. Not just the one boy named Garrett Kincaid, but a daughter, too. *Oh, Viviana.*

He ran his hands through his hair. "More than one?" He didn't understand. "How many children did she have? Are they Ed's?" This couldn't be real. "I can't imagine he allowed her to put my name as the father. This isn't making sense."

The caseworker's brow drew closer and she gave him a questioning look. "Ed? I don't know who that is. The current boyfriend was James Barrow. He is the father of the little girl. She's ten months old. He was an auto mechanic and had a job in Kerrville until about a month ago. His family lives in Houston."

He rubbed his face. "She moved on to someone worse?" Trying to figure out Viviana's love life wasn't important right now. Her children were now orphaned. What a mess, a living nightmare.

He took in one long breath, counting to seven. "Tell me what you know." He looked Sharon in the face. If what she said was correct, the boy wasn't an orphan. Garrett's stomach rolled.

No, the boy had a father, and that would be him. Maybe. Just because Viviana put his name on the birth certificate didn't mean the boy was his, but he couldn't just leave them, either. From the first time he met her at the age of ten, he had been desperate to rescue Viviana from her life. Taking her children would be a way to do that, since she never allowed him to help her.

"The boy, Garrett River, just turned five. Pilar is the girl—she's ten months old. With the birth certificate, letters from the mother and other family members' statements, we have enough evidence to immediately place them with you if you're willing. It doesn't mean you're taking permanent custody of the girl. There will be a hearing for temporary placement that needs to happen rather fast. The courts will decide on that first, then permanent in six months."

Custody and court dates? Garrett leaned back and closed his eyes. "I gave her an ultimatum. Viviana picked Ed. I left Houston, blocked her from my phone and filed for divorce." He jolted from the rocking chair and paced along the edge of the porch. His muscles jumped under his skin, restless and tight.

Oh man, what if she'd tried to call and tell him about the pregnancy? He covered his eyes with his hands, pressing the palms hard against his eye sockets. He had been so set on not allowing her to use him again. His stubbornness could mean he had left a son behind. "What do I need to do now?"

"We need you to take immediate custody of the children." She took a sip of her coffee. "Because you're a state trooper, a veteran and the state-acknowledged biological father of the first child, we could place Pilar with you if you're willing to take her. We would still have to go to court, but my hope is you agree to be the temporary solution. We still need to follow up with home inspections and parenting classes."

Looking at the horizon, Garrett cleared all thoughts and concentrated on breathing.

Torres cleared his throat. "So he doesn't need a DNA test to claim the boy? Where are they now?"

"No, as far as we're concerned, he's the father. He'll only need the DNA test if he wants to challenge the birth certificate. Right now the kids are in an emergency shelter in Kerrville. We'd like to get them out of there as soon as possible. It's not designed for the care of infants and small children. There's no one that's capable of caring for the children on the mother's side of the family, and the father's side refuses to take them."

"So you want me to take both of them."

"We do prefer keeping them together whenever possible."

He nodded. A baby needed a crib and a car seat… Well, he wasn't even sure what all a baby needed. The boy was only five. Did he need special equipment? "What timeline are you looking at for me to take the kids?"

"So you're willing to take both of the children?"

He nodded. He didn't see any other choice. If that was his son and his son had a sister, he'd keep them together. Even if the boy wasn't his son, he was Viviana's and no kid deserved to start off life that way.

Everyone was looking at him. Glancing away from

their intense gazes, Garrett turned to the horizon. This was not how he imagined fatherhood entering his life. A strong urge to pray plagued him, but he didn't even know where to start.

Sharon gave him a big smile. "Good. I know this is a shock, but the faster we can get these little ones settled with you, the better. Can you pick them up tomorrow? We'll set up a house inspection afterward."

"Tomorrow." A flash of panic constricted his lungs. Garrett turned to Torres. He was the closest thing to a friend he had in this town, but their only connections were the Marines and state law enforcement. Could he help with the kids?

No, not *the* kids, *his* kids. Hoping the sick feeling in his gut didn't show on his face, he forced a smile for Sharon.

With a warm glow in her eyes, she leaned forward and touched his hand, offering him two plain-looking folders. These folders would change his life forever. Was he ready? Could he do this? Parenting two babies who'd suffered a major trauma. He had his own issues to deal with. Nodding, he took the folders from her. "Thank you." His fingers dropped them on the table-top as if they had burned him.

He had been so careless and Viviana…oh, Viviana. He thought of the girl he had loved. His love had not been enough. Would he be enough for her children? The children were caught in a horrific trap and it looked as if he was their best hope. That didn't say much for the poor kids. He had to be stronger than his nightmares. Another wave of nausea rolled over his stomach.

This had to be made right. They needed a safe place, a home. He was all they had left. Maybe his mother could take some time off work.

Anjelica opened the door. "Do you need anything? More water? Something to eat?"

"I didn't even think to ask. I got custody of two small children, a small boy and a baby girl. Can I move them into the apartment with me?"

"Two? Not just the son?" Her mouth open, she blinked a few times before turning to the CPS worker. "Without a doubt, they'll be welcomed here. Anything they need."

Sheriff Torres nodded and turned to Garrett. "I'll talk to Pastor John. The church will make sure you have what you need. Don't hesitate to ask for help on this. Check to see if you can take some days off work to get them settled." He looked at Sharon. "He'll have the support of the community. We'll make sure he has all the bases covered."

Garrett rubbed the back of his neck. All the bases would mean childcare with his crazy schedule and appropriate gear for the kids. Food that kids ate. Did a ten-month-old baby even eat? Was she still on a bottle? *Oh man, they need psychotherapy.* He jerked his head to the caseworker, who now stood next to him. "Did they witness the incident?"

Pursing her lips, she gave him a slight nod. "We believe the boy did. Everything's in the report. Like I said, they found them in the backyard. At first the dog made it difficult to get to them. We're not sure if they crawled out before or after the incident."

And there it just went. Had he really thought things couldn't get worse?

Anjelica moved closer to the edge of the porch. "Sharon, you don't need to worry." Tenderness softened her eyes to a golden honey as she looked at Sheriff Torres. "These kids won't be alone. We can all lend a hand."

Without even knowing what had happened, she stepped up and offered her service. He hated the thought of her reaction to the fact he had a son he didn't know existed.

Asking for help went against everything he'd ever taught himself. But if he and these poor kids were going to have a chance at surviving this ordeal, that was going to have to change.

A dry throat was hard to talk around. He swallowed and managed a simple "Thank you."

Sharon smiled. "I have given you some shocking information, Officer Kincaid. In the folders you'll find my number if you need to reach me. You'll be appointed a new caseworker." She smiled at Anjelica. "Thanks for helping."

"It's the least I can do." She looked at Garrett, her wide smile tighter than usual. The new coldness burned in her usually warm eyes.

Gathering her bag, Sharon turned away from them. She stopped at the last step. "You'll make a big difference in their lives. You're doing the right thing, Officer Kincaid."

Then why did it feel like he was making the worst mistake in his life? He turned to Anjelica. "I have to go to the apartment and see what I can do to make it kid ready."

Nodding, she followed him off the porch. "You're going to need stuff for a baby. Crib, changing table, bottles, car seat, probably clothes and shoes for both of them."

The lifeline that tethered him to Earth disappeared. It was as if he was floating away from everything he knew and had no way to get back. How was he going to make this work? Halfway up the steps, he realized

Anjelica was still following him. He raised an eyebrow when he turned to look at her. "What are you doing?"

"I'm going with you. We'll need to make a list. I probably have most of what you need."

"I appreciate the offer, but you were heading into town. You don't need to change your plans for me."

She tilted her chin and looked him straight in the eye. "I'm not doing it for you. I'm doing it for those two little ones…" Lips pulled tight, she closed her eyes for a moment. "If they came to find you on a Saturday, it's an emergency situation. With me, kids always come first." Her normally open expression had a bit of steel in it as she narrowed her gaze.

Garrett sighed. "I have no doubt about that."

"I have a grandmother, a mother, sisters and cousins that will help."

He couldn't imagine that kind of large family. Of course, this morning he couldn't imagine being a father, either. Unfortunately, they didn't have any other options. Innocents couldn't be allowed to suffer because of his mistakes.

"Besides, you forgot these." She held up the two folders. Folders that he was sure told an ugly story.

He had to make this right. As much as he wanted to keep his distance from Little Miss Sunshine, he had a feeling he needed her more than he'd ever wanted, or needed, another person. He glanced behind her, scanning the fanciful farm. Especially a delicate female who seemed to live in another world altogether.

Anjelica kept her gaze hard and firm as she looked back up at Garrett. He sighed and turned his back to her, his hand resting on the wood rail. The muscles in his neck coiled. What kind of man didn't know he had a family?

Her cousin Yolanda said good looks spoiled a man. She would have argued that Garrett Kincaid was a solid man, a bit standoffish and a loner, but good. Now she wasn't so sure.

His jaw flexed as he unlocked the door. She gritted her teeth. How could men be so…so careless?

They entered the apartment in silence. He had a son and a baby daughter he didn't know about. She pulled her gaze away from his jawline and studied her hands. How could she have mistaken him as a man of honor?

Anjelica, judging Officer Kincaid won't solve any of the problems. You don't know the whole story. She knew when it came to children she had to be careful of filtering thoughts through a haze of resentment.

Holding her daughter happened only in dreams. Esperanza would have been five next month. Tomorrow's date was burned into her brain, the day she'd lost her precious baby girl. During this time, between Esperanza's death and due date, her emotions were always closer to the surface. A twist of the silver charms on her wrist helped her calm the negative thoughts.

Garrett moved to the kitchen counter that ran against the back wall. Redirecting her thoughts, she focused on him as he put the gun in a safe.

At the counter, he turned and leaned, arms crossed. His uniform stretched over broad shoulders. "Okay, enough of the silent treatment. You're bound to have questions."

"It's really none of my business." She scanned the bare room. Did he dismiss the dangers of his job the way Steve had waved off her worries of his joining the Marines? "Well, other than you're moving two children into my very small garage apartment. There's no real kitchen. And you have a very dangerous job."

The urge to scowl at him needed to be tempered. Her family lived by the rule of speaking your mind if it was helpful, kind and true. She wasn't doing a good job of it. There was always something helpful and encouraging to say, and if she tried hard enough, the right words would find their way to her lips. "What you're doing is a good thing. You stepping up and taking the kids, even if it is a little late." She bit her lip. That did not count as kind, it wasn't helpful and it might not be true. Her thoughts were going crazy.

Garrett stood across the room and stared at her, a tight, closed look on his hard face. "Do you have any questions or just observations?"

"Sorry." Okay, she needed to come straight out and ask. "You have a young son and baby daughter that you didn't know about? How does that happen?"

Leaning back against the counter again, his masculine knuckles turned white as he gripped the edge. "I'm not sure. Right now I'm feeling a bit blindsided." With his head down, he seemed to be studying his boots. "It seems the boy's mine. The girl has another father." He raised his head and looked her in the eye. "There's no excuse for abandoning a child, but I…I left town hoping to leave all my ex-wife's drama behind. I didn't know I was leaving behind a son to deal with the mess."

She didn't understand the blow to her emotions from hearing he had been married. Why would that even bother her?

With a heavy sigh, he stalked to the table and sat in one of the two chairs. Playing with the empty salt-shaker, he never looked up. Anjelica moved to the other chair and waited.

"I met Viviana in the fifth grade. She was my best friend. By the time our freshman year came around, I was in love. I spent those four years rescuing her. When I left for Afghanistan, we stayed in touch. According to her letters, she'd made better choices and gotten out of her father's house. He was not a nice man." He looked up briefly, but with a sigh he lowered his head again.

"She said she was waiting for me to return home. We met at the airport and I asked her to marry me right there." His focus moved from the simple saltshaker to the balcony door. "Looking back, I realize I had made her into a woman of my dreams. I imagined us with a home and family that even included a dog. While reading her letters, I created a life in my head that wasn't real."

Wrapping her hands over her upper arms, she tried to stave off the cold that crept into her veins. All of the letters Steve wrote her during his tour in the Middle East had been about home, too. He talked about the long hours of doing nothing. Telling her how he reread her letters over and over to get a piece of normal. He would draw pictures of the farm and the projects he planned to start when he got home. There were pages where he wrote of their daughter's future and all the kids they would raise. Her heart twisted. *Don't go there, Anjelica.*

She packed thoughts of her husband away and fixed her attention on Garrett. "How old were you when you joined?"

"Eighteen. I had just graduated and didn't have many options." He blew a hard puff of air. "The Marines were a blessing. They gave me focus and a sense of belonging, but it wasn't always easy." Standing, he rubbed the back of his neck. "I thought we were ready for the next phase of our life. I wanted to feel normal." He gave a harsh laugh. "That didn't work out so well."

Garrett walked to the French doors and opened one of them. The breeze released some of the tension that had weighed down the room. Four saxophone cases lined the wall. They were the only personal items other than a small stack of mail in his living quarters. The quietness lingered.

He reached for one of the cases. She'd heard him play several times, usually at night when he came in from work. Sometimes it was slow and soothing, other times energetic and raw, but it was always good. The music would wrap around her while she worked with the clay. She didn't feel so alone when he played.

Dropping the strap, he stared off through the French door. With a sigh, he joined her at the table. "It's hard allowing the old nightmare to resurface. A few weeks after we were married, Ed, one of her boyfriends she forgot to mention, started calling. Viviana ran to him, until he beat her—then she'd come home and I would patch her up. That had always been my job. After several attempts of trying to report him, I had to get out. At one point she threatened to tell the police I had hurt her. My career was on the line. I left. Changed my number. Deleted hers so I wouldn't be tempted to check on her. I made a clean break. I made sure she had no way to get in touch with me. If I had just left her one way to contact me…" With his elbow on the table, he pressed his forehead into his palm.

She heard resentment in each word. If his ex-wife had hidden the boy from him, he had every right to be angry. "Why are you taking the girl, too? It sounds like there's a chance the boy is not even yours. Why did they come to you for placement?"

"I guess we were still married when she gave birth, so my name is on the birth certificate and there's no one else." He shrugged. "As a little girl, she had dreams of living in the county with lots of animals." He snorted. "I promised her I'd make her dreams come true. Maybe I can make good on the promise with her children. Also, I'd guess there is a fifty-fifty chance the boy is mine. I couldn't take one without the other—she's his baby sister. Can you imagine how much he would hate me if I didn't bring his sister home with him?" He scanned the room and blew out a hard puff of air.

She still struggled with the idea of not knowing about a child and then taking in two. "Where's their mother now? Why have they been taken from her?"

His jaw did the tick thing again and he nodded to the two folders she had set on the table. "Everything about them and their mother is in the folders." He shook his head.

Picking up one of the folders, she flipped it open. "You haven't seen the children?" It was the baby girl. Her heart melted at the big eyes, perfect tiny lips and tons of tight curls that surrounded the sweetest face. "Oh, Garrett, she's adorable. Look at her."

As if wearing a neck brace, he turned and gave the eight-by-ten photo a quick glance. With his attention back on the door on the opposite wall, he nodded. "She looks like her mother." He moved away. "For now, I should clean out the office so it can become their room."

"What happened? How'd she lose the kids? What about the fath...?" She flipped to the next photo. Shocked by the scene, her stomach heaved. The folder fell from her grasp. She leaned over and braced herself. "I'm gonna be sick."

Garrett rushed to her side. He muttered under his

breath as he pulled her hair back. "Do you need the restroom?"

Forcing in deep breaths, eyes closed, she shook her head. "No, I'm fine now."

"I should have warned you the crime-scene photos might be in there." He went to the mini refrigerator and pulled out a bottle of water. "Here." He pressed the cold plastic into her hand.

Sitting up, she leaned her head back. She adjusted her scarf. Knowing horrible things happened was one thing; seeing them in pictures was a completely different story. How was she going to get that out of her head? "Oh, Garrett, those poor babies. We have to help them."

Garrett pulled the other chair next to her and placed his hand on her shoulder at the base of her neck. "I'm sorry. I should've looked through them before letting you see the folders. I was…just avoiding."

"Were they in the room? Did they see what happened to their mother?"

"The boy might've been." He was so close she could hear his breathing. "Pilar is a baby and, hopefully, won't have any memory." Leaning back, he pushed his hair away from his forehead.

With the folder in hand, she was careful not to look at the bloody photos, instead focusing on the picture of the little girl and her information sheet. "Her name is Pilar Rose. She just turned ten months old." Making sure to breathe, she reached for the second folder.

Hand flat on the folder, he spread his long fingers over it as if to protect her from the contents. "I just want to see him." She held her hand out for the deceptively plain folder Garrett covered. "I'm prepared now. I was caught off guard. Let me see them."

Instead of handing over his son's file, he opened it.

She kept her gaze on Garrett's face as he stared at the top photo of the little boy. He blinked several times and his throat worked up and down. Not able to resist, she peeked over his arm and saw a serious little boy with Garrett's green-gray eyes staring back at them. He was a little darker with a mop of curly hair, but other than that, she was looking at a young version of the man sitting next to her. Garrett pressed his hand over his eyes.

She moved back, wanting to give him space to collect himself. Two breaths in, one hard breath out. Counting the steady rhythm gave her something to focus on instead of asking questions. He was breathing with his whole body. A broken heart was nothing new to her, but to watch such a controlled man fighting to hold it together made her want to wrap him in her arms.

The hard muscle along his jaw popped. This time, instead of wanting to scowl at him, she wanted to comfort him. Fisting her hand in her lap to keep from running her fingers along the tense muscle, she fought the urge to sooth him.

After a long while, he slid his hand down his face and covered his mouth, looking up at the ceiling. She saw moisture on his eyelashes. He handed her the photo, paper-clipped to an information sheet. Scanning the sheet gave her somewhere safe to look. "Garrett River Kincaid Jr. He has your name."

"And apparently everything else, too. No DNA test needed. It's like looking at an old picture of me as a kid." He stood but didn't go anywhere. The silence grew tense.

She didn't know what to say, so she tossed a few words around. "He has curly hair." *Well, that was a stupid thing to say.*

"I had curly hair as a kid, too. When I went to school,

my dad shaved it off so I wouldn't look like a girl. It came back straighter." He lifted one hand and ran it through his own thick hair.

The neat cut was now unruly, but she still couldn't imagine him with curls. "The kids in my family all start off with ringlets, too, but around five or six they lose them."

"I don't know how to do this, being a father."

"We can make it work." She blurted it out. Thinking of what happened to those two small children, she knew they needed a home full of love and good memories. Tears started burning her eyes. "We have to make this right for them. We have to bring them to a real home."

He took his eyes off the bare walls and looked at her. "We?"

"I won't let you *not* let me help." She hugged the folders.

The obstinate man lifted an eyebrow at her.

She gritted her teeth and pressed the folders closer to her chest. With one deep breath, Anjelica looked back at him. "Okay, so I didn't word that very well, but you get my meaning. They need more than food and a bed to sleep in. They need consistency, a home filled with love, and you need help."

"Right now they need a safe place." He disappeared into the smaller room he was using as an office.

She hadn't been up here since he moved into the garage apartment. There was nothing on the walls. The bookshelf remained empty. A brown sofa and a small round table with two chairs had been provided in the rental. He hadn't added anything of his own, not even a TV. The only personal items were the saxophone cases. Not a single picture of his family or friends.

Garrett came back into the living area and sat a

laptop on the table. "He's five and she's ten months old. What am I gonna need? Maybe I should make the smaller room my bedroom and put them in the bigger room." He looked up at her. "Or does a ten-month-old need to be in a room with an adult…a parent? I work nights sometimes and if there's an emergency…"

The color left his face.

"Garrett, you'll need someone to watch them when you're at work."

"I'm going to call my mother. If she could move here, that could work. I can sleep on the sofa. I've had worse."

She had a bad feeling he was going to be stubborn about taking help. "I have some baby stuff. It's all un-used. I have a crib, high chair, changing table, rocker and the smaller stuff like blankets."

He rubbed his eyes and stared at the screen.

"You need some sleep."

He checked his watch. "I'm fine."

She reached over and pushed the top down on his computer. "Get some sleep. I'll have the things they need by the time you wake up."

She took a deep breath and smiled. Could she do it? Could she hand over all of Esperanza's furniture? She closed her eyes and felt the peace wash over her. Garrett's baby girl needed a room full of love, and Esper-anza didn't.

It was time. She opened her eyes and smiled at Gar-rett. "God provides."

He sighed. "Not sure about God, but I'm not your problem to fix. I do need some sleep, but I don't have a lot of time to waste to get everything ready for…"

"You have enough time to sleep. I'm telling you, al-most everything you need is close. Okay? When you wake up, come over to the house."

Yes, it felt right. Maybe this was why she hadn't cleaned out her baby girl's room yet. God knew Garrett would need it.

Chapter Two

An explosion rattled the walls. Garrett jerked straight up from sleep. No, not an explosion, just another nightmare. He threw back the heavy blanket and sat on the edge of the bed. Avoiding the frayed braided rug, he made sure to plant his bare feet on the cold tile floor. Taking several deep breaths, he anchored himself in Clear Water, Texas. In the present. Sand blew against the roof. Grinding his back molars, he buried his fingers in his hair. Not sand. Afghanistan belonged in his past. The thin glass in his window shuddered under the force of the violent wind outside.

The sound that had woken him penetrated the room again. Not in his head, but outside. A hefty storm was making a fuss and building power. Barefoot, he left the bedroom and walked across the apartment. The security light keeping it from being too dark to see. Opening the French doors, he stood at the threshold of the small balcony. Tiny bits of hail had collected on the deck. A few minuscule chunks pelted him. His thin T-shirt offered little protection from their sting.

He blinked, confused by a cloth flapping in the desert wind, twisting around a group of kids playing soccer. His fingers closed around the iron railing. It was cold, hard…real. He inhaled, pushing his lungs to their limit. With eyes shut, Garrett fought to get his mind back to the here and now. *I am standing on my balcony in Clear Water, Texas.*

It had been a while since he'd had this type of episode. Maybe the news he'd gotten today was part of this mixed-up nightmare. He was taking full responsibility of two kids. He knew firsthand no matter what you did, bad things still happened. Another boy's smiling face and bright dark eyes came to mind. Counting breaths, he shook his head.

His mind latched on to the present, and he opened his eyes again. This time, he made sure he saw Anjelica's backyard. Even in the dark he could still make out the miniature farm surrounded by ranches that gave the illusion of endless hills and trees. A cry came from the area of her large garden.

A bedsheet? Okay, that was real. Why was that crazy woman chasing a bedsheet across her yard in the middle of a storm? He didn't even have a sense of time. He glanced inside and saw the clock, which read 10:33 p.m. He had slept longer than he'd planned.

Shaking his head, he grabbed his trench coat and slipped on his boots. With his hat firmly planted on his head, he made his way down the stairs of the garage apartment. He knew she was a bit on the fanciful side, but this was strange behavior even for her. She had no business being outside with hail and lightning. Did she have a death wish?

By the time he walked through the gate, she was balanced halfway up the deer-proof fence, attempting to untangle the sheet from the eight-foot corner post. Her bare feet were precariously poised on the tie bar between the huge cedar post and the stay. Her new fluffball pet leaped about and barked.

"Bumper! Stop it!" She tugged at the sheet. Anjelica's long dark hair was plastered to her like a second skin, making her look more like an elf. Even standing on the tie bar, she couldn't reach the top of the corner post. Did she notice the hail? Cutoff sweatpants exposed her golden-brown skin to the elements. He shook his head as he cut across the tilled garden.

The dog finally caught the edge of the white sheet between its teeth. "Bumper! No! Bad girl! Let go!" As she tried to pull the sheet away from the Yorkie, Little Miss Sunshine lost her balance.

Garrett rushed to catch her. She landed in his arms with an "Oomph." Lightning streaked across the sky as he ran for her covered back porch. He counted the seconds between seeing the flash and hearing the thunder. Five seconds. Too close for comfort. His arms tightened their hold when she started wiggling. "Hold still or I'll drop you." She might be small, but she struggled against him with toned muscles.

He leaped up the three steps and under the eclectic collection of ceramic wind chimes that lined her porch. Their musical notes sounded angry tonight.

"No! No, I have to cover the bush! The hail's gonna destroy it."

"You don't have any shoes on, and even small hail can be dangerous." Once he had her bare feet on the boards, he looked into her large eyes to check their dilation for signs of a concussion. Her irises were so dark he couldn't see her pupils in the dim light.

Maybe she already had brain damage. Another bright light flashed, and for a split second he could see everything as if it was high noon. He saw a thick heavy scar that ran across the base of her neck. The soft edge disappeared into her hairline by her cheek. Then he was blinded again just as quickly. Was that why she always wore a scarf?

She tried to push past him. "I've got to cover my plant before it's destroyed."

The ceramic chimes thrashed in a sudden gust of wind, and it was hard to hear over all the noise. "No, stay here." He made a gesture to her head and feet, hoping she understood. "I'll cover the plant."

Pulling his hat low, he ran back into the storm and crossed the yard to retrieve the sheet. The dog followed, leaping and barking like they were playing a game.

"Bumper, get back here," Anjelica yelled from the top step. The undisciplined dog ignored her.

With one hard yank, he had the sheet down. The two-foot bush had already lost some of its early growth. Small leaves dotted the ground. Using the wind to help, he threw the sheet over the top of the plant. Then Garrett looked around for something to anchor it.

"Here, use these." Anjelica ran past him to pick up some red bricks lining the bottom of the fence. At least she had mud boots and a hat on this time, along with a bright orange scarf wrapped around her neck.

The pelts of hail grew harder. He tucked his head and drew his shoulders higher. He was apparently as crazy as his landlady.

The dog pulled on the sheet, tossing her head back and forth with a growl. The furball could fit in his pocket but fought with the fierceness of a lion. The pink bow did nothing to soften her attitude.

"I've got this!" Garrett pointed toward her porch, hoping she would follow his command. She shook her head and moved to the base of the bush with a brick.

"Bumper! Stop!" The dog darted away from Anjelica and grabbed another corner.

Garrett scooped the bit of fluff up in one hand, holding the pup out of the way while he tucked the heavy sheet around a brick with the other, making sure it was under the bush and tight enough to stay in place.

On the opposite side of the shrub, his tiny landlady crawled out from under the plant and put her hands on her hips. "I think that'll do it," she yelled before finally running back to the safety of the deep porch.

He followed. One step behind her, he tried to shield her from the worst of the storm.

Once on the porch, she threw her beat-up hat on a bench, then sat on a worn rocking chair and pulled off a boot. She wore two left rubber boots. One of them had colorful stripes, but the other one was purple with white flowers all over it. Yep, she lived in another world altogether.

"Glad you found proper footwear."

Waving a delicate hand toward her yard, she said, "This wasn't in the weather report. I couldn't find my boots when I realized it was starting to hail." She pulled off the purple boot and dumped water out of it. "My only thought was to get to my Esperanza. It just started sprouting spring leaves."

She never made eye contact as she flipped her hair over her shoulder. Wet, it looked black. Instead of the usual colorful blouse, she wore an oversize faded purple T-shirt with Fighting Angoras Football printed across the front. "I know it sounds irrational, but I just wanted to cover my plant." With a deep sigh, she stood. "Thank you so much for coming to the rescue, but I guess that's what you do. Rush into danger like a good soldier." She stood and took Bumper from him. The little dog started licking her face. "You know, now that you're a father, you'll have to be more careful."

His eyebrow lifted high as he stared at her. "Did you really just call me out for being in this storm? I wouldn't be out in the storm if you had stayed inside."

She blushed and looked away. "Sorry. I'm not feeling very rational right now." With the back of her free hand, she wiped at her eyes.

Oh, please don't cry. He scanned her cluster of outbuildings and enclosed pens behind the garden area, a mismatched collection of painted structures that housed chickens, rabbits and goats. She was the mayor of a miniature village for all the misfit farm animals in the county, and now he was adding two children to the mix. He shouldn't be surprised she had easily agreed to him moving the kids into the garage apartment. She collected damaged goods. "Looks like everyone else is safe from the storm." That should make her happy.

She rewarded him with a smile. Nodding, she kissed the top of the silky mop's head. "My dad bragged he built those to withstand a tornado."

The hail was larger now, dime-sized nuggets zinging off the tin roof like ricocheting bullets, putting his nerves on edge. He took a deep breath. He was in Clear Water, Texas. Far from war.

At least tornadoes were rare in the Hill Country. He took off his own hat and slapped it against his leg. Chips of ice clattered to the wood flooring. Calling the weather in Texas unpredictable was the definition of understatement.

It wouldn't surprise him if he found a few bruises in the morning. He pushed his hair back. The little froufrou dog ran over to him and put a paw on his muddy boot. The clipped tail wagged so hard its whole body squirmed. "Bumper?"

Anjelica smiled at the wet rat. "I found her just the other day on Bumper Gate Road. I put an ad in the local paper, but no one's come to claim her."

Standing in front of him, she moved in for a hug before he realized what she had planned. "Thank you for saving my plant. I do think you'll do a fine job as a father."

His jaw clenched. He had never been a touchy hugging kind of guy, but he'd been hugged more times in the few months since he'd moved to Clearwater than he had his entire life. He remained still, not wanting to offend her by pulling away.

Kids liked hugs, too. He remembered wanting to be in his mother's lap, but she had always been too tired or too busy. He managed to lift an arm and give her a pat on the shoulder, hopefully not too stiff. She shivered in his arms. They were both cold and wet. "You need to go inside and change."

She backed up and grinned at him as if she'd made a new friend. "Thank you, Officer Kincaid. Um, now that you're a father, you might think of a less dangerous job?"

He frowned. "I like my job."

Another flash of lightning. He counted again, one Mississippi, two Mississippi, three Mississippi. A golf ball of solid ice landed at his feet. He narrowed his eyes and then looked at the path back to his apartment. The trip back to the garage wasn't far, but with that last bolt of lightning, he doubted it was wise to run across the yard again. He looked at his watch. It had taken him a couple of hours to go to sleep, but he had been out for seven hours.

"Officer Kincaid—"

"Call me Garrett."

"Oh!" She grabbed his arm. "Now is as good a time as any to show you the baby equipment."

She leaned in closer, and the smell of vanilla and earth intrigued his nose. The lyrical sound of her voice tickled his ear. "Promise not to tell my parents I was outside in this weather. My mom would have a fit and Papa would tell me to move back home, again. They wouldn't like that I'd go that far for a simple shrub."

He had a feeling there was nothing simple about the shrub.

"Come on." She turned and opened the screen door.

Garrett followed her and crossed over the well-trodden threshold. In his line of work, he'd been in about every kind of housing, but this was straight out of a children's picture book. Alice's rabbit hole had nothing on this girl.

It was everything his apartment wasn't. The old farmhouse had a huge kitchen. A family of ten could easily sit at the table.

Even though the cabinets were painted white, splashes of color touched everything. More ceramic creatures hung from strings, while others lined the windows and cabinets.

"Sorry about the mess. I made a big batch of tortilla soup earlier tonight to share with my grandparents and a few other people in town. Then an idea struck, and I ended up in my ceramic studio before I cleaned. Have you eaten since lunch? Here, let me get you some." Without waiting for his reply, she loaded a ceramic bowl with the aromatic soup. Fresh herbs and spices filled the kitchen. His stomach grumbled in anticipation.

She pulled a spoon out of the dishwasher and moved to the table. "Here, sit down and eat. I'll slice an avocado and heat you up a corn tortilla. What do you want to drink? I have milk, sweet tea and water."

"Water's fine." Before he got the first spoonful of soup to his lips, she had a small plate with avocados and thin corn chips on the table next to him. Another trip and she handed him a warm tortilla and a tall glass of ice water.

"I'll put some in a container for you to take to the apartment for later." She set a blue bowl on the counter, then dug around in the cabinets. "I'm the only person that lives here, and I still can't find a lid." Pulling out a red one, she held it up and smiled at him. "Found one." She snapped the red lid onto the blue bowl.

Of course she did. Why start matching now? "Please sit and eat with me."

With the dog bouncing about her feet, she sat down across from him. She slid the plastic bowl his way.

"Thanks." He dunked the tortilla into the warm soup. He didn't want to waste time with forming more words. He had fallen in love. He closed his eyes and savored the rich flavors on his tongue.

"I'm the one that's grateful. Thank you for braving the storm and helping me cover Esperanza."

He opened his eyes. He really shouldn't have been surprised by anything she said. "You name your plants?"

She smiled again, but this time it was a little tighter, not as bright. "It's an Esperanza plant, the same name as my daughter. I planted it as a memorial for her."

Great going, Garrett. "Well, it's a beautiful plant. And a beautiful name. It means hope, right?" He cleared his suddenly dry throat. "Looks like we covered it in time."

Maybe he should leave…instead of staring at her like an idiot. Obviously, she no longer had her daughter. The baby stuff she said she had, it must have been… another reminder that children couldn't always be protected from bad things. And now he was responsible for two who already had a tragic backstory. He took a deep breath and set the spoon down, his appetite gone. "Thanks for the soup."

"I'm glad I had it here for you. Are you finished?"

A nod was all he managed. She took everything to the sink. The lights flickered as the thunder rolled through the house. She tilted her head toward the ceiling. "Doesn't sound like it's letting up." The lights wavered again. "Follow me—I'll show you the baby stuff I have ready for you and Pilar." She walked through an archway that took them into a living room. Several mix-and-match sofas and chairs made for a welcoming room. He was surprised by the white sofa. The red floral sofa he expected, but the white one? How did she keep it clean? He didn't know anyone who actually dared to have white furniture. Red, white and blue pillows and blankets were everywhere. Yellow flowers were tucked into odd containers all over the room. It looked well lived-in, the site of years of family events and memories.

"I've been wanting to tell you how much I appreciate you playing the sax on the balcony. When I'm working in the studio, I open my door to listen. You should come to church with me one Sunday. Pastor John is really into music. Did you ever play in a band?"

He nodded and followed her around the furniture that looked as if they'd been salvaged from an old barn. "All through school, and when I joined the Marines, I played for them, too."

"Wow." She stopped in front of a floor-to-ceiling bookcase and looked up at him, making him feel taller than his six-one. "I would have taken you for a football player, you know, the warrior type. I don't think of soldiers as musicians. Do you play any other instruments?" She tilted her head as if trying to recalibrate what she knew about him.

"I was a total band geek, marching and jazz. I play some strings, too, but I prefer the sax. I didn't get any size on me until later in high school—I wasn't a jock." He cleared his throat. She looked as if she wanted to add him to her collection of odd animals now.

He glanced at the shelf behind her, and a wooden display with a folded flag caught his eye. The flag sat above some medals and a picture of a young Hispanic male in dress blues. Next to that was a wedding picture. A very young Anjelica in a white wedding dress standing in the arms of the same soldier. Letters were etched into the wood: Estevan Diego Garza.

She turned and looked behind her. "Oh, that's my husband, Steve."

"He was a marine, too." *Way to go and state the obvious, Garrett.*

"Yes, one of the heroes that didn't come home." Graceful fingers touched the picture. "Being a hero was his life's dream. He planned to become a firefighter or EMT when he got home." A bright flash flooded the room in blinding light. Then everything went dark and silent.

He reached out to touch her arm, but the lights were on again and she had her happy face back in place. "I'm sorry. I'm going on and on. You're here to see the baby stuff." A few steps and she opened a white painted door.

Nerves started crawling again. Garrett's skin became too tight for his body. The urge to escape and go back to his simple rooms had him feeling edgy. There was nothing wrong with beige. Beige was calming, very calming. A peaceful color for kids who needed a quiet place to heal. He liked quiet places.

Concern in her eyes, Anjelica placed a gentle touch on his arm. "Are you okay?"

She was the one who'd lost her soldier and a baby, but she was worried about him?

"I'm good. We need to get this settled so I can figure out the next steps I need to take to make this right."

"Garrett, it's not your fault the way things played out."

A corner of his mouth twitched. She actually had him smiling. "I don't think that's what you were thinking earlier."

"Guilty. Sometimes we dive headfirst into conclusions and judge too fast. Sorry. So are you ready to see the stuff?"

"Lead the way."

Anjelica stood at her daughter's door. She had put so much planning and time into decorating this space. Each step had been documented and sent to Steve, along with images of her growing belly.

Five years ago, she spent hours in that rocking chair, crying until every part of her body ached. After a while, she was able to visit the room without crying. The sadness was still there, but softer. The last few months, she kept telling herself to call her mom and sisters so they could help her pack it up.

Now she knew God had another plan for this room. "Garrett, most of what Pilar will need is here." She turned on the overhead light and waited for him to join her.

In the middle of the room, she stopped and took a deep breath before she turned back to him. "This would have been Esperanza's room. Nothing has ever been used."

Garrett stood in the doorway and scanned the room with a slow steady movement. "I can't take your stuff from here."

"Why not? I was to the point of packing it up. It was made for a little girl. Everything your daughter needs is waiting for her."

His head jerked up. "She's not my daughter." Both hands dug into his hair, interlocking the fingers at his neck. With his head back, he closed his eyes and blew out a slow waft of air. "I guess by tomorrow she'll be my daughter." He closed his eyes, his jaw working twice as fast as before.

She wanted to put her arms around him and soothe the pain. Instead she stepped away and placed her hand on the quilt draped over the rocking chair. Buela had made the blanket. "Garrett, you can do this. I think God brings people into our world that need us and vice versa. It's been heavy on my heart that all the stuff was being wasted." She walked to the white crib that was tucked into a colorfully painted cove that had once been a closet. Pink and green triangle flags hung over the bed. "Please let me give it to Pilar and your son."

Confusion marred his strong face as he watched her. "Why are you doing this? What do you get out of helping us?"

Adjusting the blankets they had picked out so long ago, she smiled at his cynicism. "I can't save every child out there, but I can help you save these two." If she wasn't careful, she was going to cry. She feared he would misunderstand and this could all fall apart. She stiffened her spine as she turned and glared at him, making sure not to show any weakness. "Stop being so suspicious and say thank you."

He walked around the room. Touching the rocking chair, setting it in motion. He saw the bags full of new supplies and clothes. "What's this?"

"While you were sleeping, I called a few of my family members and ladies from the church. They gathered some stuff you'll need for the children."

In front of the chest of drawers, he stopped and looked at the wall.

She had painted *Esperanza* across the upper part of the wall, surrounded by stars and butterflies. The whole room was decorated with flowers and friendly critters, a little secret garden.

With a frown, he stared at the wall. "You painted this?"

A nod was all she managed.

He moved to the window and held the wispy sheer curtain to the side so he could look out into the storm. Wind slammed the rain against the window.

"I called my mother."

Disappointment should not have been her first reaction, but it was. She had started thinking of them as a team when it came to these two kids she hadn't even met yet. "Oh, so she's coming to help? You don't need me, then."

He rubbed his face. "No." He looked away, staring at the mural. "She hasn't returned my calls. It looks like I'll need someone to watch the kids. A temporary fix for now. Until I can get a place of my own and make permanent arrangements." He turned back to her. "Is there anyone in your family you recommend?"

"Me." Before he could form any words to argue against her idea, she rushed on to explain. "I've been thinking about this all day. I'm a sub at the school and I volunteer with the group home. I know what these babies have been through, so you wouldn't have to explain that to someone new. I can stop taking sub jobs and you can pay me the same daily fee, but I would be available day or night."

He looked back out the window. Lightning flashed. She forced herself to breathe and waited for him to process the options.

Well, she tried to wait. "I also had another idea. Please, listen and think about it before you respond. I think you and the kids should move into the house. It's bigger and I can live in the apartment."

She chewed on the inside of her cheek while waiting for his response.

"No." He crossed his arms. "I'm not kicking you out of your family home."

"You're not." Hands planted on her hips, she tilted her head. "The garage is part of my family home and I actually lived there as a teenager once."

"No. We'll stay in the apartment. It's fine. I'm not moving into your house."

"Okay. Then what about hiring me as your baby-sitter?" She smiled. "I do think it's important to have someone that can watch them with your crazy hours. I can be right there at a moment's notice. The next best thing to a live-in nanny. I always wanted to be Mary Poppins."

He didn't say anything. He stared at her with the muscles flexing in his arms.

She broke eye contact first and rearranged some of the pillows. "You don't have to worry about taking the kids anywhere or waiting for someone to get here. It's perfect, right?"

"I don't like asking for help."

A giant eye-roll threatened to pop from her head. *Stubborn men.* "You didn't have to ask for help. I'm offering. My heart is hurting for these babies. I'm so sorry your mother isn't coming, but I think this will work out well for the children."

He sighed. "It's funny if you think about it." He leaned across the crib, picking up a stuffed ladybug. "This morning I didn't even have a girlfriend. Now I'm talking about baby furniture and hiring a nanny. Seems I skipped a few steps from bachelorhood to fatherhood."

The sadness in his eyes ate at her heart. "God has placed these kids with you. It's going to be okay."

He sighed. "Are you sure you want to take us on full-time? I have a feeling these will not be well-adjusted kids." He gave her a lazy, lopsided grin. "I know I'm not well-adjusted—I'm barely housebroken. I don't even know what a normal family should look like."

"Well, the one thing I'm an expert on is family, and first let me tell you, there is no such thing as normal. Believe me, I know." She could not hold back any longer; she walked over and hugged him. His frame tightened as if in fight-or-flight mode. She held him gently until he relaxed and gave her a stiff pat on her shoulder. "Garrett, I want to help those sweet kids."

The muscles in his forearms bulged. Head down, he backed away from her. "They might not be so sweet." Then he nodded, his face relaxing. "Okay, so I have a stocked nursery and a nanny. This might work." He looked up. "Thank you, Anjelica." Halfway to the door, he stopped. "What about the boy? I need to get him a bed, too."

"I can call around, but if nothing comes up, we have a couple of bunk beds upstairs." She brushed past him to cross the living room but paused in the doorway. The smell of earth after a rainstorm crossed her senses. Closing her eyes, she absorbed the scent. It was rich and dark.

"Anjelica?"

Jerked out of her own head, she jumped forward and bumped into him. Large hands steadied her. "Are you okay?"

Looking up, she saw the concern in his eyes. He looked that way a great deal when around her. He probably thought she was a complete flake and maybe he was right.

"I'm fine. We can move all the stuff in the morning." She rushed past him. She needed some distance. That was it. Other than her family, and the one date she'd had with Jake Torres, she hadn't been this close to a man in a long time. She'd forgotten how good they smelled, and how different they were compared to her.

"Can I use your restroom?" he asked.

"Sure—right through that door." She pointed to the right of the staircase.

Standing in the middle of the living room, she lost her purpose. What was she doing?

Anjelica went back into the kitchen. Bumper barked, demanding attention. The little Yorkie looked like a rat just rescued from a flooded river. Anjelica grabbed a towel and rubbed down the little dog. Garrett and Steve seemed to have a great deal in common. Why did some men want to rush into danger?

Buela and Mom were always on her about getting back into the dating scene. She knew it was time. But not with Garrett. He had too much on his plate already.

The biggest problem was his job. He was a lawman and she didn't see that changing anytime soon.

Talking to the dog, she made her way to the studio off her kitchen. "Just because I married one soldier doesn't mean I want another one in my life. No thank you." She held Bumper up so they were face-to-face. "Next time around, I want a man with a nice safe job. Maybe I should warn Garrett about the matchmaking duo. Now that he's a single father, I'm sure they have bumped him up on their list." She chuckled. This might be fun to watch, because it was not going to be her. Nope, his job was too dangerous for her peace of mind. But she was ready to date again.

In a few months, she'd be twenty-five. On her wedding day, she had imagined life with Steve in five and ten years. He'd be back home full-time, and they'd have two or three kids. She rubbed the little dog's head and sighed.

Si Dios quiere. Her parents had taught her that saying for her whole life, to trust in God's will. Sometimes it was easier to say she trusted in God's will than live like it. The wind rushed against the wall and slammed the screen door. Hail hit the roof harder and the storm whirled around the old house.

Loud banging made her jump. The wind played games with her outdoor furniture. She rushed to the door.

Garrett gently caught her by the arm. His hard face looked even sterner. "You can't go out there." His voice sounded like a growl. "It's even more dangerous than before. It's late anyway—you should go to bed."

She narrowed her eyes and pulled her arm out of his light grip. With her hands on her hips, she lifted her chin. "I outgrew a bedtime a few years back. What about you?"

The wind manhandled the hundred-year-old oak

trees around her yard. The sound sent chills up her spine. She sucked in a large volume of air as she looked out the window. The force of the storm pelted the hail into the passageway. The rain came in at such a slant, looking as if it could slice through skin.

With muttered words under his breath, Garrett pushed her farther into the kitchen. "Is there a room without so many windows?"

"My studio." Bumper barked and jumped around her feet. "There's just the garden doors, but I have shutters over them. It's in there." She pointed to the door on the other side of her table. "But my animals. What—"

"They have shelter." He opened the door, flipped on the light and peered in. "This is good." He took her hand and pulled her inside the studio space and closed the door.

Sitting on the wooden bench her grandfather had carved, she patted the empty spot next to her. His big frame took up the rest of the space, long legs stretched out in front of him.

Total chaos reigned outside. She often thought of the wind as a gentle lullaby at night, but not now. It expressed itself like a two-year-old in a full-blown temper tantrum, a giant two-year-old. It sounded as if trees were being tossed around.

Bumper buried her head under Anjelica's arm. Her heart slammed against her sternum. "Dear God, please keep everyone safe." Thunder rolled, but in the studio they couldn't see the flashes of lightning. The walls rattled. The lights went out, plunging them into darkness. "Oh no, I left candles in the kitchen."

"We'll be fine. It shouldn't last long. We're safer in here in case any furniture or branches get tossed into one of your windows."

Another clap of thunder was followed by a loud crash. This time the whole earth shook. An explosion sounded too close. Had something hit the house? Blood rushed to her ears. "What was that? Oh, my babies have to be scared."

His long fingers found her hand and took hold. "It's okay. Good thing about Texas is the storms never last long. So this is your grandparents' house?" His voice reached out to her, low and soothing.

She knew he was distracting her and she let him. "My great-grandparents had the property and a small house. My grandparents started this house and added on and updated as the family grew. They wanted to move into town and have a smaller place, so they sold it to Steve and me."

As quickly as the wind had started, it was gone, the silence heavy. Anjelica held her breath and waited, but she couldn't even hear the rain anymore. "Is the storm over?"

He squeezed her hand. "Stay here while I check the damage." He stood. He flipped the switch, but the room stayed dark.

"I'm going with you."

He frowned and opened his mouth, then shook his head. "Stay close to me. There could be lines down. We don't want to rush out and make things worse. Trees and structures could still fall."

Bumper squirmed in her arms. "Let me put her in the washroom and get the flashlights."

As they exited the back door, she gasped. Her world had been turned upside down. She prayed she'd find everyone safe and sound.

Garrett's warmth and solidness comforted her. Looking around, she found most of the rocking chairs and some of her wind chimes were missing. Broken pieces of ceramic projects littered the ground. Frantically scanning for the piece celebrating her wedding and then pregnancy, she didn't find it. It was her favorite, whimsical shapes and swirls with sunflowers, frogs and butterflies in an asymmetrical layout.

She gasped. Large pieces of it were scattered across the porch. She found one of the frogs on the bottom step. She picked it up and ran her thumb along the jagged edge where the leg had been.

Garrett rushed to her side. "What is it? Are you okay?"

She nodded. "Sorry. It's one of my wind chimes. I started this one when we bought the house. Each section was tied to a memory." She made sure to smile at him. "It's just an object, right? The memories are in my heart. Let's make sure everyone's all right. That's the important thing. Not broken pieces of clay."

"Are you sure?" He looked back at the porch. "Was it the one with the big sunflower and bugs?"

She had to laugh. "Yes, butterflies, ladybugs and frogs. Steve loved frogs. He always had a pet one growing up. He wanted to put a pond for frogs on the property. I didn't want the cleanup or risk to children. I was going to decorate the nursery with frogs if we had a boy." She closed her eyes and gathered her thoughts. "I'm sorry—this doesn't matter."

"Do you want to gather it up?"

"No, it… We need to take care of my poor babies."

The beams of their flashlights scanned the area. Debris, both natural and man-made, cluttered the yard. As they walked past the empty garden, she let out her breath with a sigh of relief. Her pens and outbuildings all stood strong. He followed her to each shed and helped her check the huddled groups of animals. Everyone was safe and accounted for. Her father would be proud of his work.

Garrett's phone went off. Glancing down, he pulled his lips tight. "I need to go. We have low water crossings that need to be barricaded." He glanced at her little farm. "Everyone is safe for now. You stay inside until we can get someone out here to look deeper at the damage."

He turned to the garage and stopped. There on the roof they found the reason for the loud crash.

The old hackberry tree had moved into his bedroom. Thinking of the possibilities, she felt her heart skip. "I'm so glad you came to my house."

He gave a dry laugh and shook his head. "There has to be irony in this somehow. I just inherited two homeless kids and now it looks like I'm homeless, too." He rubbed the back of his neck.

"No, you're not. I think when you said no to my offer of the house, God wanted you to say yes."

"You're joking, right?" He looked down at her.

She shrugged and gave a halfhearted laugh. "Maybe. But you have to admit my plan is sounding better now."

"I'm still not kicking you out of your own house. Where would you live?"

"I can move into town. You could have a fully furnished house. We don't even have to move anything."

"No. I couldn't live in your house while you live somewhere else. I'll call Sharon and tell her I need more time before I pick up the kids."

"We can't let those babies stay in emergency care. If you refuse to live in my house, I could call my family and have the roof fixed in less than twenty-four hours. You know there aren't a great deal of rental options in

Clear Water." She tucked her hand into the bend in his arm and leaned in close. *"Si Dios quiere."*

"Did you just say he wants God?"

"No. It's a saying that means to trust in God's will. My grandmother and mother say it all the time. It's drilled into my brain. *Si Dios quiere.* It's how I try to live my life. The worse things get, the more I lean on that trust."

"I don't trust easily." He was looking straight ahead. The muscle in his jaw popped. "My son probably doesn't trust men at all. Will you go with me? I'm sure they have issues, too, and men would be on the top of the list. You, being the nanny, might help them feel safer."

"I would love to."

He nodded and patted her hand. "Okay. Don't worry about the roof." He waved to the apartment. "I'll take care of it after I get off work."

"You don't worry about this." She made a bigger wave. "You worry about rescuing the good people of the county and I'll take care of my property. You are about to discover the power of the Ortega army. Be very happy we are on your side." She gave him her best wicked laugh. "My father and brothers will have all this cleaned up and fixed before you can drive your patrol car around the county three times."

He looked at her one more time. "Are you sure you're okay?"

"Yes, I'm stronger than I look. I promise." She'd learned the hard way how strong she could be. Now she hoped she was strong enough to make the right choices for her heart. She wasn't sure how much more it could take.

Si Dios quiere. I'm trusting You, God.

Chapter Three

Anjelica looked at her hands clasped tightly around the handle of the bag she had packed for the two little ones they were about to take home. Garrett pulled his truck into the empty parking lot of a nondescript brick building. It didn't even have windows on the front, just one glass door.

During the forty-five-minute trip to town, she told her heart not to get too engaged. These were his children. His family, not hers. She was just the nanny. But still, the pictures of those innocent faces embedded themselves in her head. She had a feeling that in the end, her heart would be broken again. She was never the kind of person who could keep an emotional distance. With her, it was always all in or not. How did someone teach their heart portion control?

Garrett cut the engine. He leaned over the steering wheel and looked at the sky. "I can't believe how fast this has happened."

"You made it easy for her to move the kids from an emergency shelter to a home. I'm sure she wishes all her cases were this easy." She checked her watch again. "We're early."

With a glance to the backseat, he opened the top button of his starched blue shirt. His black cowboy hat and jeans looked sharp. "Well, I guess it's time to fill those car seats." He cleared his throat. "Thank you for all you've done so far."

"How could I not help?" Waiting for him to move out of the truck, she sat in silence. Her attention went to her watch again.

Thirty minutes early. If he needed to sit out in the parking lot, she could do that, but she really wanted to see the kids.

"Okay." With one hand on the door, he turned to her. "Are you ready?"

She bit back a laugh and just nodded. He was a mess. She imagined a first-time dad might react the same way with the birth of his child. But for him, skipping those first few years probably made it harder.

The heat off the black asphalt threatened to melt her makeup. Garrett held the glass door open for her as he pulled on his collar. "It's unusually warm for March."

Nodding, she entered a sterile and empty lobby. Green vinyl chairs lined a paneled wall. Above them were posters depicting women and children, along with warning signs of abuse or neglect. A narrow corridor led to rows of more doors.

Without any hesitation, Garrett started down the hallway. At the far end, Sharon and an older man stepped out from one of the rooms. "Oh, Officer Kincaid, you're early. Good. The children are here. This is Joe Ackerman. He's your new caseworker."

The men shook hands and everyone else was introduced. Half of the wall behind Garrett was glass, so they could clearly see inside what looked like a conference room.

The man stepped back through the door and spoke with a woman who stood inside holding an infant car seat. A little boy sat in an oversize chair, his feet dangling above the floor as his small hand hung over the side of the yellow blanket covering the baby.

Anjelica touched Garrett's arm. Looking down, he raised his eyebrows at her. She pointed to the brother and sister. "There they are." Not sure why she was whispering, Anjelica shifted her gaze between the man standing next to her and the little boy who looked so much like him.

His forearm tensed under her hand. He stopped talking and became still. Nothing moved.

Sharon broke the silence. "Are you ready to meet them?" She turned to look at the kids.

Garrett took in a deep breath. He licked his lips and his throat worked as if he were trying to swallow. Anjelica wanted to wrap him in her arms.

Sharon continued talking, apparently oblivious to his struggles. "He attended the Head Start program. We know he can speak Spanish and English, but he hasn't spoken since they've been in custody. They documented that his oral development is behind, but that isn't unusual for a dual-language child. Pilar is physically behind. She's not sitting up on her own yet. There are small developmental delays, but they look to be more environmental." She sighed and looked back at the kids. "He's protective of his sister and gets very upset if he can't see her. There are several signs of general neglect."

"Such as?" Garrett asked without taking his eyes off the children.

"He knows how to make her bottle and dress them both, and he can work a microwave. We have found him changing her diaper. For a five-year-old, that indicates to us that he was the caregiver."

Had she just heard him growl?

Anjelica's fingers tightened around his arm. Garrett's other hand came up and covered hers.

"He's been appointed a child psychologist. He's experienced a traumatic event and will need time to heal and feel safe. You'll need patience in large supplies." She looked at Garrett and smiled. "I'm so relieved you're letting us place Pilar with you. I'm not sure Rio would survive being separated from his sister."

Garrett nodded. "Rio?"

"At Head Start they called him Garrett, but we've discovered his grandmother called him Rio. The rest of the family called him River. What do you want to call him?" Sharon looked through the window at the kids.

Garrett shrugged. "We could ask him what he wants to be called. If he wants Garrett, I'll go by something else. Can we go in now?"

Oh no. I'm not gonna cry. Anjelica let go of Garrett and squeezed her fingers together in front of her. With a count to five, she steadied her heartbeat.

He paused with his hand on the door. "What do I say?"

Sharon gave him a soft smile. "Keep it simple. I'll introduce you. But still tell him who you are and what's going to happen in small steps. Don't lie or make promises you can't keep."

With a nod, he walked through the door. Anjelica followed but hung back, staying close to the wall. She needed to proceed slowly. This was his time to bond with the kids. As much as she wanted to hold that baby girl, she was only a temporary babysitter. The hired help.

The mini Garrett tucked his feet under himself and

hovered over his sister. His curly dark hair hung in his face, hiding his eyes. The baby appeared to be asleep. She looked too small for a ten-month-old.

Anjelica watched as Sharon and Garrett approached the little boy. The small body froze, becoming unnaturally still. He didn't look at them directly but from the corner of his eye.

Anjelica held her breath. She couldn't even imagine what either were thinking. Would the boy trust Garrett? Would he be healed from this ordeal, or was he permanently wounded?

Garrett went on his haunches so he was eye level with his son as Sharon introduced them. After a brief smile the young women handed him the car seat with the baby inside, but he couldn't take his eyes off Rio.

He studied the features of the little boy. Wayward curls framed the small face. Each feature perfect and delicate. He was so tiny. His own father's words buzzed across his brain for a moment. Telling him he looked more like a pretty little girl than a boy. His father would laugh in front of his football-watching buddies and say the dog made a better son. He narrowed his eyes. No, he wasn't going there and *his* son would never be shamed like that.

Body locked in place, Garrett didn't make a move, not even daring to breathe as he looked at the miracle that sat before him. A boy who looked like him, a boy who was part of him. How could he not have known?

So much time already lost. How could this wounded little guy who didn't know him ever trust him? All his son knew was that a man now calling himself his father had abandoned him, had left him behind.

The boy continued to ignore him.

"Hi there. My name is Garrett River Kincaid, just like yours. I knew your mother. We went to school together." Nothing. "I'm your father and I'm here to take you home."

Mini Garrett made a whimpering sound and moved closer to his sister. Garrett sat in a chair and pulled the blanket back from the sleeping baby. "It's gonna be okay. Your sister is coming, too." Garrett had no idea what to do. He looked at Anjelica. Back against the door, she was still standing on the other side of the room.

He looked at the boy, who was fiercely trying to cover his sister. The easiest and fastest action would be to pick them up and put them in the truck, but he remembered being a kid and not understanding what was going on around him. It had been terrifying.

Pulling a chair closer to his son, he looked to Anjelica. "Why don't you join us?" As she slowly moved to them, he turned back to his son. "I want to introduce you to the woman that is going to help take care of you and your sister, but I don't know what name you want to use." The boy didn't acknowledge anyone in the room but kept his gaze on his sister.

"Your mom called you River? She always loved my middle name. Did you know there was an actor she liked with the same name?" The boy's lips stayed taut as he focused on his sister. "What about Garrett?"

A heated glare briefly made contact with Garrett under the dark curly hair that hung across the boy's forehead. Garrett fought the urge to brush it back. He was pretty certain that the boy wouldn't be comfortable being touched. "Okay, I'll take that as a no. I'm told your grandmother called you Rio. That's clever, using the Spanish name for *river*. Do you like Rio?" No response.

Frustrated, he looked to Anjelica for help. She

shrugged and leaned forward to look at the infant. No longer sleeping, the baby girl blinked at them. *"¿Puedo recoger, Pilar?"* Without taking her gaze off the little boy, she patted Garrett's shoulder. "I asked if I could hold his sister."

Garrett grinned. "Yeah, I speak *poquito* Spanish." He measured about an inch between his thumb and index finger. In simple Spanish, he reassured his son that Anjelica was a nice lady who loved babies. "She has an *abuelita*, too."

For the first time, Rio looked away from his sister and glanced between them, acknowledging their presence with a scowl.

She smiled at Garrett. "I recognize that look." Turning back to the little boy, she smiled. *"¿Rio, Puedo recoger, Pilar. Por favor?"*

The big brother nodded and pulled the blanket off his sister. Anjelica reached down and unbuckled the strap, then gently picked the baby up. Pilar was too tiny and fragile to be healthy. As she cradled the infant in her arms, a look of total bliss covered her face. Garrett's breathing slowed. He knew, without a doubt, she would love these kids in ways he couldn't.

A tiny hand reached out and took the edge of the yellow scarf Anjelica wore today. "Hey there, sweet girl. Are you ready to see your new home?"

Home. He would be taking them home. He looked around for some water. His throat had gone unbearably dry.

A touch on his shoulder caused him to jump. Sharon stood there. He'd been so absorbed with the kids and Anjelica that he'd forgotten Sharon was in the room. Not good. They needed him to be on top of his game. He couldn't afford to get distracted.

"I have a few papers for you."

He placed the empty carrier on the floor and rolled his neck. "Sure. I have some questions about the dates for our court hearings." He looked down at the little boy, who had all his attention on Anjelica. "Rio, I'm going to talk with Ms. Sharon. Anjelica will stay here with you and Pilar. Then we'll take y'all to your new home."

After a moment of being ignored, Garrett joined Sharon at the other end of the long table. As she explained the process and timelines again, he kept glancing over at the little family he was about to take home. They were his responsibility now.

Anjelica sat at the table next to Rio. She was softly singing to them, gently brushing the baby's face and playing with her small fingers. He tried to figure out what he was feeling, but he got nothing. How had he ended up here? *God, I hope You have a plan because I got nothing.*

Anjelica looked up and caught him staring at her. If there was a picture of perfect motherhood, it would be there, Anjelica. He almost snorted when he realized God had already answered his question. Yes, there was a plan and He had put Anjelica smack in his path. Okay, so maybe he was going to look a little deeper into trusting God.

"Garrett?" Sharon closed the folder. "Do you have any questions?"

"So after a few months, I can apply to adopt Pilar?"

"Well, yes, but you don't have to rush into anything permanent."

He had to admit he was surprised by the feeling of protectiveness he already had for the girl, and he hadn't even held her yet. "She doesn't have anywhere else to go, and I'm pretty sure the best way to make my son hate me forever would be to separate him from his sister."

She chuckled. "Yes. For now, let's take the first step. Get the three of you settled. The first court date will have to happen fast because of the emergency situation."

"Speaking of getting us settled, what happened to the dog that was with the kids in the backyard?"

Rio looked up, his face becoming animated as his gaze darted between the adults. That had gotten his attention.

"She was taken to the pound."

"What do we need to do to pick her up?" He looked at Rio. "Do you want to get your dog?"

His son didn't answer but jumped from the chair and pulled the diaper bag off the table.

"I'm not sure you—"

"It's my son's dog. We can pick her up on our way home. The dog helped protect the kids." It should have been him standing between his son and the violent mess of Viviana's life. "We're not leaving her in the pound."

With the strap over Rio's shoulder, the bag dragged on the floor as he headed to the door. He stopped and stared at them. An expression too stern for a five-year-old hardened his face.

"I'll call the shelter and let them know you'll be claiming the dog."

"Thank you." Joining Rio, Garrett reached for the bag. "I'll take this. We have new car seats for you both in my truck."

Anjelica adjusted Pilar on her left hip and held her free hand out to Rio. His son glared at her and pressed his back against the wall.

"Rio, walk with us. *Por favor.*" She kept her hand out and waited with a smile on her face.

Garrett held the door open. "If you want to come with us to get the dog, you'll need to hold her hand." After a silent moment, the small hand slipped into Anjelica's. With a heavy rock in the pit of his stomach, Garrett followed his new family to his truck.

Surreal was the only word he could think of as Anjelica smiled at him over her shoulder. She carried his daughter on one hip while holding his son's hand. His children. What was he going to do now?

Chapter Four

Garrett checked his rearview mirror again. They were still there, secure in their seats. He couldn't see Pilar. Her car seat faced backward, right behind him. With the blanket Anjelica had packed over his head, Rio sat on the opposite side of the truck. Seeing himself in the boy was still a bit bizarre, and the kid had some strange behaviors.

He chuckled. There were times he wanted to hide under a superhero blanket, too.

Between the car seats, a big spotted Catahoula cow dog stretched out. Her head rested on Rio's arm. Her white coat with large black spots was covered in gray and brown smaller specks. She was a beautiful dog.

The unrestrained joy at the reunion between boy and dog tugged at his heart. Even now, the big dog hardly took her focus off her boy. Engraved on her dog tags was the name Selena.

Memories of Viviana and him listening to the late artist flooded his mind. It had been one of their go-to albums whenever life got too hard. Viviana would dance and sing along to "Bidi Bidi Bom Bom" until he laughed. She would sing in Spanish at the top of her lungs, trying to get him to sing along. They would finish by slow dancing to "I Could Fall in Love."

Had she chosen that name because of the connection to him, or was he reading too much into a dog's name?

Now the dog eyed him with a suspicious glare, but then again, he might have been reading his own insecurities in the mixed blue and brown eyes.

It was clear she would hold out judgment on him. He could hear her say she'd trust him for now, but mess with her little humans and his life was over. He owed this Selena an extra treat. Life had gotten harder for his son than it had ever been for him. He'd had a charmed childhood compared to his son's.

Instinct told him he had a son who suffered from PTSD. If a preschooler could suffer from post-traumatic stress, he would think seeing your mother killed would do it. No telling how many fights he had witnessed or heard. The real question was, could he provide the kid with the help he needed so he wouldn't be scarred for life?

"So are you going to share?" Anjelica crossed her arms and raised an eyebrow.

His eyebrows knotted. "Share what?"

"I want to know what you found funny. I could use a chuckle, too, but you're all grim and serious again. So I guess it's over."

With a nod to the backseat, he turned onto the country road that would take them to Anjelica's home. His home. "Just thinking that disappearing under a superhero blanket sounds like a good coping strategy to me."

Garrett hit the brakes harder than planned, pitching everyone forward. Rio's blanket fell. As the little boy grabbed it with one arm, he reached for his sister with the other.

Cars, trucks and a church van filled every area a vehicle could park around Anjelica's house. He saw Pastor John and a couple of teen boys carrying a soggy mattress from the side of the garage. Two baby goats played with a couple of laughing kids along the side of the house.

He slowly pulled up to the gate. The De La Cruz twins, Adrian and George, waved at him from a truck loaded with debris that now carried his bed, too. The quiet property he had started to think of as home had been invaded. Music played somewhere in the backyard.

Yesterday, while he helped with a couple of water rescues, only Anjelica's father, a couple of brothers, Adrian and George, along with Pastor John, had shown up to help repair the roof. As the sun started to peek over the hills, they'd all shown up again, plus Sheriff Torres. Now it looked as if the whole county was hanging out on Anjelica's little farm.

The plan had been to move the kid's furniture into his apartment while they went to pick up Rio and Pilar.

"Oh, Garrett. I'm so sorry. I knew my dad and brothers had called in a few friends to help with the apartment, but I didn't know they would invite the whole town."

"What's going on?" Scanning the property, he frowned. He wasn't sure he understood what had occurred since he left.

"Well, I called Mom about getting some of the things you needed that I didn't have, and, well…that means she called Aunt Maggie, who in turn called the family and church members."

She looked at him with apprehension on her face. "They want to help. Between getting the kids here, cleaning out the apartment and setting up for them, we didn't have time to get it all done. I wanted to have everything ready. So…um, I called."

"She called church members?" His stomach flopped a bit. While he was in Kerrville picking up his new family, the whole town had learned what a screw-up he was. "I'm not much into people knowing my business."

Her eyes softened. Leaning across the console, she touched his arm. Warmth seeped through his shirtsleeve. "It's not like that. They really want to help. I mean, don't get me wrong." A soft chuckle broke the tension in the cab. "In Clear Water, the story is across the county before you finish telling it." She patted him on the arm. "But this way, we tell them what we want them to know and they're not making up crazy stories."

Knuckles tight on the steering wheel, he watched people come and go between the house and garage. "The story is crazy."

His jaw popped a couple of times. With a shift of his gaze, he looked at the backseat. Rio had pulled the blanket back over his head and the dog rested on his leg.

"I don't want people looking at the kids as if something is wrong with them."

What he really wanted to do was hit something. He needed to do something physical, to shake this restlessness off his skin.

One call and she had a whole town at her doorstep. Anjelica's family, most of whom he didn't know, were helping without asking why. His mother hadn't even returned his calls yet.

Envy was not a pretty emotion. He glanced at the people moving around the house.

He wasn't sure why he wanted to talk to his mother so badly, anyway. Gina would remind him of all the ways he'd messed up again. If she refused to help him, he would have to rely on Anjelica and her family even more. Acid burned his stomach.

Some of the women standing on the porch waved when they noticed them parked on the road outside the gate. He didn't have a great deal of experience with families other than Viviana's. Hers always involved drama. He hated drama.

Yeah, he really needed to go for a run before he exploded, but he didn't have time. The days of going for a long run whenever he wanted no longer existed.

He hadn't been this edgy since he first returned from Afghanistan. He rubbed his palm over his eyes. "I can't keep using you and your family to help me with my problems."

With a cute tilt to her head, she smiled. "Are we back to that? At the very least, this will give you enough time to find the perfect place to make into your permanent home, if that is still what you want." She glanced behind them and checked the sleeping Pilar.

Lowering her voice, Anjelica kept her focus on the baby. "Garrett, you don't want to be moving the kids from house to house, just making do. They need stability."

As he eased the truck into the driveway, his jaw started to hurt from biting down. With a deep breath, he forced each muscle to relax.

His instinct yelled not to take their help, or maybe it was pride. Sometimes the difference between the two was hard to find. Pride might come at too high a price if it cost the kids' well-being.

A soft touch pulled him out of his thoughts and brought his full attention back to her. The warmth of her touch went through his shirtsleeve.

With one click of a button, she rolled down the window. The sun's reflection exposed gold-red splashes in her hair he hadn't noticed before now.

He turned away from Anjelica and scanned the green valley surrounded by hills coming alive with spring growth. In her world, family always helped when needed.

"I'm sorry," she said again.

He snorted. "For your family or my mistakes? Not your problem, but your family is here to help. You're right. We couldn't have gotten it all accomplished in such a short time. The faster I can have the kids settled in the apartment, the better. We need to thank them for their help."

"Garrett, it's not your mistake the way things played out."

With the Tahoe in Park, he gritted his teeth. He hated crowds. They couldn't be comfortable for the kids, either. Adrian De La Cruz waved at them as he drove his work truck full of debris off the property.

"I appreciate the help, but I'm thinking this will be overwhelming for the kids, especially Rio."

"You're right." She glanced at the backseat again. "I'll have Mom clear out the house and send everyone that's not working on the apartment home. I know they want to welcome your new little ones. We're just used to hanging out with each other." She leaned in and squeezed his hand. "Everything gets turned into a party with them, but they'll understand."

He wished someone could explain it to him because he sure didn't understand any of this.

Checking on the kids again, he saw a small hand poking out from the blanket. Rio patted the dog, even though he hid. Wanting to hide from the world, he understood.

How was he supposed to help these kids when he

was on the verge of losing it himself? The cabin in the woods overlooking the river would have kept everyone away, but now the world knocked on his door in the form of two innocent babes.

Garrett rotated his grip around the steering wheel, twisting the braided leather.

"Garrett, are you ready?"

No, but there wasn't much choice. "Yeah, you get Rio. He seems more at ease with you. I'll carry Pilar."

"I can go ahead while you wait in the truck and clear them out."

"No, the kids need normal, and for you this is normal. We need to thank them for everything they've done for us." Normal? He would follow her lead because he had no clue. He did know it wasn't normal to scan for snipers or explosive traps. He had to tell himself that these were the Ortegas, and they weren't going to harm the kids.

Pushing his lungs to their limit, he stepped out of his SUV and onto the unsteady ground of a new world.

"Do they show up unannounced often?" He moved to the passenger door behind him and opened it. In his truck, a baby who now belonged to him slept.

From the open door on the opposite side, standing next to the covered Rio, Anjelica smiled at him. "To them, family just shows up when needed. They do seem to have adopted you." She grinned. "Really, I'm so sorry. The concept of personal space is foreign to them, especially when they have a mission."

"Mission?" With a gentle unsure touch, he removed the straps of the car seat.

"Oh, Garrett, I'm sorry to tell you, but you and your new family just became mission number one."

His head came up fast and he hit his head on the edge

of the door frame. He closed his eyes and pinched the bridge of his nose. Spots danced behind his eyelids.

"Are you okay?"

He nodded. "Great, now I'll have a headache."

"Relax." She winked at him. "I promise most of the time they're harmless. They'll clear out fast." She nodded to the little boy, who was pretending to disappear. She tugged at the blanket. "Rio, this is your new home. There are some people that want to welcome you, but they won't be staying. They just want to say hi." The blanket hung over her shoulder, but Rio kept his eyes closed. He had Selena's long leash in a tight grip.

A crowd had gathered on the front porch. Everyone had huge smiles on their faces as they waited.

He looked at Anjelica as she made her way to his side. With her free hand, she squeezed his arm. "Are you sure you don't want me to go in and ask them to leave?

"It's going to be okay." Maybe if he said it enough, he would believe it.

With a sigh, he picked up the sleeping Pilar. The strangeness of holding her was already giving way to a peaceful wonder. Her lax body molded to his hard frame, her soft cheek pressed against his shoulder.

Trust and love given without asking. He took in the smell of baby shampoo in the thick curls of her dark hair.

The easy acceptance that made her feel safe enough in his arms to sleep scared him a bit. Picking up the diaper bag from the floorboard, he glanced at his son. The now-familiar glare worried him. How was he going to make this work if his own son hated him? Had he scowled at his father the same way?

He tried to pretend they were not being watched by a bunch of people he didn't know.

With his free hand, he reached for his son to reassure him they were in this together.

Rio jerked his shoulder out of Garrett's touch and turned his head away from him.

Anjelica patted Rio's back. "Come on—let's go check out your new room. My mom and Buela, along with a bunch of cousins and friends, are waiting to say hi."

The little boy leaned back and took in all the people standing on the porch. He narrowed his eyes and then looked back at Anjelica. She gave him an encouraging smile, then turned it on Garrett. "You'll both be fine, and Rio will learn to trust you. Just give him time."

The not trusting was a survival skill his son had unfortunately had to develop. The kid had a great deal to get over before he would trust Garrett.

"I know you have an *abuelita*. I have one, too. We call her Buela." She nodded. "She wants to meet you and Pilar. My mom and cousins, too. Everyone here is very nice."

He pulled back and made a whimpering sound. The dog gave a low rumble of a growl.

"This is too much for him." Maybe he should tell everyone to leave now.

The front door opened, and the screen door banged shut. From the side of the house, Bumper came running, followed by leaping and kicking baby goats. She started barking and dancing around Anjelica. A cold sweat coated Garrett's skin and his breathing became labored. At the end of the leash, the Catahoula's hair stood along her spine as a low growl rumbled from her throat.

"Bumper! Stop it." Anjelica picked up Rio and balanced him on her hip, then scooped up the energetic dog with her free arm. "Shh, be nice. Rio, this is Bumper." Bumper stretched her neck out and licked Rio's

ear. The little boy giggled. Selena reared up on her back
legs with her front paws on Rio's leg. She pushed her
nose between her boy and the fluffball of a dog.

Tension tightened Garrett's muscles. A dogfight
could break out with Rio and Anjelica stuck in the middle, and he had Pilar in his arms. He wouldn't be able
to react fast enough if he needed to.

Bumper barked and Selena's tail wagged as Anjelica patted her on the head. She chuckled. "Look, Rio,
they're already friends." She made eye contact with
Garrett. Her eyes gleamed. "This is a good sign. Everything's going to be all right." She smiled at Rio. "Ready
to see your new home?"

He leaned over and checked out the people on the
porch again. Looking up at Anjelica, he gave her a sol-
emn look and a slight nod. Garrett had not been able
to get any response from the boy—well, unless glares
counted.

*God, I know I haven't talked to You much, but it
seems I really need some guidance with this little guy.*

With Rio on one hip, Anjelica released Bumper to
the ground and took Selena's leash from Rio.

This is it. Garrett followed her again. She waved at
the women on the porch. That seemed to be the permission they needed to swarm. Before he blinked, they
were surrounded.

He couldn't keep an eye on all of them at once.
Someone touched his shoulder from behind. He jerked
around. Pilar lifted her head and gave a soft cry.

*Breathe, Garrett. Breathe nice and easy. No one
here is trying to harm the kids. You are in Anjelica's
front yard.*

Anjelica's mother led the pack. "We hear congratulations are in order. What a shock, right? So we are throw-

ing you a surprise baby shower and home-warming party all at once." All the women laughed.

He worked to keep the panic off his face; he could play it cool. Something must have slipped, though, because Anjelica looked at him with concern. He tried to smile and reassure her he was fine, but it felt a little forced.

"Mom, I'm sure all he wants right now is to get the kids familiar with their rooms and settled."

A small herd of children ran through the yard, disappearing into the house.

He couldn't do this.

Anjelica wanted to protect Garrett from the wave of people, but she learned long ago to go with the tide. It went much smoother that way and you got out faster. She knew they meant well, but they didn't seem to understand someone not wanting them in his life.

She glanced at Garrett. This had to be a bit alarming for a man who sought solitude. Less than a day and his world had been turned upside down. Her heart went out to him as he tried to take it all in stride.

"Officer Kincaid! *Como esta?* How are you?" Buela cupped his jaw and kissed the cheek opposite the sleeping child. "They have worked very hard and the apartment is almost done! Praise God, in time for your new family."

"Como esta, Buela?" Anjelica greeted her grandmother.

"Muy bien. Good, good." She went to her granddaughter and cupped Rio's face. "So tell me who this fine boy is."

"Rio, this is my Buela and my mother." She shared a smile with the older women. "This is Garrett River

Kincaid Jr., Garrett's son and Pilar's very brave brother. He goes by Rio."

He tucked his head against her shoulder, closed his eyes and started sucking his thumb.

"Hello, Rio. We heard how very brave you were to save your sister. This will be a great home for both of you and your dog. Big dogs love living in the country."

Her mother hugged Garrett, then placed a hand on Pilar's back, her hand going up and down on the small rib cage. "Oh, *mijo*, your daughter is precious."

"Mamma, this is very nice that everyone's here to greet us, but I think it might be overwhelming for the kids." Rio had tried to pull the blanket back over his face but just managed the corner. She refrained from pointing out that Garrett had gained a slight green tint to his skin.

Anjelica couldn't help but think she should get Garrett his own superhero blanket.

"*Mija*, they are almost done with the apartment. While everyone is clearing out, let's visit the playroom we set up for the children while they are with you."

Taking Garrett by the hand, Anjelica led him through the sea of women. He muttered a few thank-yous as they crossed the yard.

The other women backed up, making a clear path to the front door.

"Oh, we're so sorry." Aunt Maggie was standing on the steps. "We wanted your children to feel welcomed."

"We didn't even think about all the newness of this for the poor lambs." Yolanda joined her mother.

Words swirled around them. She noticed Garrett taking deep breaths through his nose. Pilar stiffened and started fussing again. He patted her back.

With Rio still on her hip, she led Garrett up the steps and to her house. Vickie held open the door.

"Thank you." She turned to Garrett. "This is Vickie. She's married to Sheriff Torres."

With a nod to the woman, he followed Anjelica and Rio into the living room. The smell of fresh cinnamon rolls from the oven filled the air. Garrett adjusted Pilar and whispered to her.

With the door closed to the chaos outside, there was an unobtrusive peace in the house. The baby reached for his nose and smiled at him. Her heart melted as Pilar made the sweetest gurgling, and Garrett smiled. Some of the color returned to his face.

The door opened. Pulling the baby close, he turned to face the intruder. It was her mother, her sisters and Buela. Her tiny grandmother clasped her hands together. "Come on. Before we check out the apartment, we can show Rio the playroom in my house.

Eyes closed, Rio had gone into stealth mode.

"Garrett, these three are my younger sisters, Mercedes, Esmi and Jewel," Anjelica said.

He nodded to each of them as his large hand supported the back of Pilar's head. He moved next to Anjelica. "We'll just have to show Pilar the playroom, since we can't find Rio."

Anjelica smoothed the boy's soft curls. "I hope he likes trains and basketball." She leaned forward and kissed his forehead. "If not, he'll need to let me know what he likes. I hear he has a bed that looks like a car."

Her mother placed her hand on Rio's back. "It's been a long day for everyone. Let's get everyone out of the yard, then we can show you your new room in your dad's apartment." She leaned in close to Garrett. "All the women are cleaning up and clearing out."

"Thank you, Mamma. We can give Pilar a tour of the house. Buela said the apartment was almost finished. Will it be ready for them to sleep in tonight? I could fix a room upstairs."

"They'll be ready tonight. Just the final touches."

Buela waved her hands toward the kitchen. "Dinner is warming in the apartment oven."

"We thought about setting it up here, since this house was meant for a family, but the babies' main home will be in the apartment with Officer Kincaid, right? You should have switched houses." Her mother gave her a pointed stare.

"Mother."

Garrett's gaze met hers across the room. The panic seemed to be climbing back into the mist of his green-gray eyes.

She wasn't sure who needed comforting more, Rio or Garrett. Well, Garrett was a grown man. A man she didn't want to be attracted to. She couldn't let his vulnerability convince her heart to look at him as anything other than her boss. The screen door opened, and her youngest brother, Philip, popped his head in "I was sent to tell you that they will be ready upstairs in another fifteen minutes."

Chapter Five

❧

"Good, we have time to see the playroom." Buela had apparently had enough talking and marched out of the room, not even questioning if her troops would fall in line. Like a good private, Garrett followed her.

Adjusting Rio to her other hip, Anjelica moved next to him and leaned in close. He had to tilt his head to focus on her soft voice and not the scent of vanilla and spice.

"I'm so sorry. She looks all sweet, but she is kind of a bully. She tends to take over." She looked up at him and smiled.

He decided not to point out she was always trying to feed him and had even jumped in to rearrange his life without his asking for the help.

Jewel laughed. "Yes, a tiny bully with good intentions, but a bully nevertheless."

Crossing the living room to the nursery, they passed four kids sitting around the coffee table, coloring. Bumper was curled up between two of the girls, her short tail thumping when she saw him. Selena had not left Anjelica and Rio's side.

With a deep breath, he trailed the women. There had

to be something for him to do, something to move or fix. He'd have joined the men working, but it didn't seem right to leave the kids with Anjelica so soon.

Six women crowded the room, staring at a man on a ladder. Tiny clothes covered every surface.

"Look at this one." The sheriff's wife, Vickie, held up a mini dress in pink camo print, drawing everyone's attention. Daddy's Girl was printed across the front. "Isn't it the cutest?"

The knot in his stomach pulled tighter.

Maggie Shultz, one of the aunts, was opening packages of little towels and putting them in a basket. "We were just organizing the chaos before leaving. Most of these things will be moved to the kids' room in your apartment. We decided to stick with the secret-garden theme. Is that okay?"

Was she really asking his opinion? "Sure." He couldn't imagine a baby would even notice.

The man with paint in his hair started down the ladder. "It's done." He stepped down and reached a hand out to Garrett. "Hi. I'm Gary, a friend of Pastor John's. I was asked to add *Credo* and *Amor* along with *Pilar* and *Rio* to the wall. Anjelica said she wanted *Faith* and *Love* along with *Hope*. I did some work upstairs first so it would be dry by the time they moved in." He nodded to the baby on Garrett's shoulder. "We cut it pretty close."

Yolanda put a stack of clothes she had been folding in a dresser and hugged Anjelica. "It's beautiful. How are you doing with all the changes?"

"I'm good. It's time." After one more nod and a tight hug, Yolanda turned to him. "This must be a jolt to the system. From bachelor to suddenly having two children in one weekend."

Understatement of the year. "Yes, ma'am."

"Please, call me Yolanda. I don't understand how a woman could not tell a man about his children." She patted his arm. "Anjelica told us about your mother not being able to help."

He shot a glare at his nanny. Was she going to be telling them everything?

She looked worried. "I told them she was working and couldn't get off with such short notice."

"It's understandable. I'm sure she'll come as soon as she can." Buela stood in front of the newly painted wall. "Gary, you're truly gifted." She turned back to the group. "Now, Officer Kincaid, you must have no worries. You have us. If there is one thing Ortegas are good at, it's taking care of kids. Had eight myself and raised twelve." She moved to Rio. "No worries for you, either. Pilar will have many sweet dreams in her new room upstairs."

The artist gathered up his paints and said his good-byes.

Garrett watched him leave with longing. "Maybe I should check on the apartment before we take Rio and Pilar up there?"

"Let's put a blanket on the floor so Pilar can stretch and play. She's been in the car seat all day. And you can see what the men are doing." Leaning down, Anjelica put Rio in front of a large basket full of toys. "Rio, pick some toys for your sister." With a job to do, Rio started digging through the basket.

The little girl blinked a few times and looked around the strange room. Her arms tightened around his neck when Anjelica went to remove her from his arms. His heart twisted and he placed his free hand on her back. "It's okay. I've got her."

Anjelica nodded and petted the back of the soft curls.

"She already trusts you. That's good, but she needs floor time to build her strength."

He moved to the blanket on the floor and laid Pilar on her tummy, but she fussed a bit. "I can take her with me."

Yolanda had a strange seat-looking thing. "This will help her sit up." The women took over, gently pushing him back. Rio gave her toys.

Garrett stood at the door for a while and watched as Pilar smiled at her brother. The women encouraged the brother and sister with their praise.

Hesitant to leave, he backed into the living room. Glancing out the front window, he noticed most of the cars were gone. The house did seem quiet...quieter than it had been when he arrived. The little dog sat on the pillows as if waiting to be served. As he walked past her, she jumped down and followed him.

Moving to the back door, he found the sheriff, Jake Torres, and Pastor John in the kitchen.

The pastor held out his hand. "The apartment looks great. My guess would be better than before with the De La Cruz twins on the job. Couldn't help but notice a nice collection of saxophones. I take it you play?"

"Yes, sir."

"We have a solid band at the church, and the family likes to play. You'll have to join us sometime."

"Thank you for helping with the repairs."

"Hey, Kincaid." Torres shook his hand and then pulled him into a shoulder bump, finishing it off with a couple of hard pats before he stepped back. "The apartment looks great. You're staying here and Anjelica's watching the kids. Sounds like a perfect fit."

"I think it'll work for now. Thanks for helping." The sheriff had grown up in Clear Water. He would know more about Anjelica's husband. "Torres, did you know Steve Garza?"

Tight-lipped, he gave a sharp nod. "Anjelica's husband? Sure. He was a few grades behind me in school. Good kid, a bit reckless sometimes, but he never meant any harm. They got married the week after graduation. He enlisted and was killed his first tour in Afghanistan." Torres gave him the look. "She's special to us."

The pastor nodded. "She has a tendency to give and not allow others to help her." He cleared his throat. "We're a close community and would hate to see her taken advantage of by someone she's helping."

Garrett gave the men a quick affirmation. "Duly noted, but she is a bit forceful in her offer of assistance. She really hasn't given me much choice."

Both men chuckled. The pastor grinned. "She's an Ortega. I'm married to one and know them well." He patted him on the shoulder. "Sorry—they will come in and try to take over your life. But their plans are all for good."

"Two kids and a storm already messed up any plans I had managed to make."

Jake Torres nodded. "You know what they say about plans."

Garrett raised an eyebrow. He really had no clue.

Torres put a hand on his shoulder. "You make plans and God laughs."

"Yeah, well God's having a grand old time with me, then."

Anjelica's grandmother joined them. "You gentlemen look up to no good."

Pastor John hugged her. "Officer Kincaid was just saying how impressed he was with the Ortegas' fast-moving organization." With an arm around the small woman, Pastor John turned back to Garrett. "You have to thank the little general here." He nodded to the matriarch of the Ortega family. "When she mobilizes the Ortega army, anything can get done." He winked at the blushing grandmother. "She's a great friend to have on your side." He turned back to Garrett. "I'm going to gather up the boys I brought and take them for the pizza I promised. We'll be praying for your new family."

"Thank you."

Jake gave him another hug. "You're doing a good thing here, keeping the kids together. Don't hesitate to call." Jake stood back and stared him straight in the eye.

Garrett nodded and tried not to break eye contact. He was afraid that as a fellow marine, Jake saw too much. Jake narrowed his eyes. "Call for any reason, even if you just need to talk. I also know a man who works at the VA named Reeves. He's been there. Easy to talk to. Don't try to do this alone."

Garrett smiled and nodded. "Got it. Thanks for all the help today."

"Not a problem."

Vickie came into the kitchen with the now-small group of women. She wrapped an arm around her husband. "Hey, missed you." She gave him a quick kiss. The town sheriff and former marine laughed. "Missed you, too."

Anjelica, her mother and a couple of other women giggled. Someone muttered, "Newlyweds."

Everyone started talking at once. Garrett couldn't keep track of the conversation, but they didn't seem to have a problem.

Man, how did people keep their sanity with big families?

He focused on Anjelica. She was talking to her

mother. "I am more than capable of making dinner for a small family. I cook large dinners all the time." Frustration replaced her usual cheerful smile.

Some of the ladies agreed with her, while others started arguing.

Buela held her hands up. "Ladies, please. You're giving poor Officer Kincaid a headache."

"What about me?" the sheriff asked.

"Oh, Jake, you're used to us!"

"And on that note, I'm out of here. Call at any time, Kincaid."

"Now, *mija*," the tiny grandmother said, taking charge, "we know you are more than capable of fixing dinner for a whole mess of people. But there will be two scared babies under your care and a brand-new father. They need your full attention, so let everyone pitch in and help Officer Kincaid by providing dinners for the first week he has the children. Everyone wants to help. You should let them."

Anjelica's face softened. "You're right, as always, Buela." She kissed her grandmother's cheek. "Okay, Mamma, sign people up."

Maria Ortega turned to him. "Do you have any preference or anything you don't eat?"

He shook his head. "You really don't have—" Her glare cut off any argument he might have thought he had. "No, ma'am. I eat whatever you put in front of me."

She smiled and nodded. "Good. Your mother did well. Okay, we are out of here. You both get some rest. You're going to need it."

And with that, they were all gone. "Let's get the kids from Jewel and take them to their new home."

He followed her back to the playroom. His pulse picked up as Pilar lifted her hands to him. Her grin did him in. This was why he'd sacrificed his serene one-man existence. Now he needed to prove he deserved her trust.

"I think she wants you."

Rio crossed his arms and glared again.

"Hey, little man, the look's getting old. Come on—get Selena and let's go upstairs." If he kept after it and stayed the course, Rio would open to him.

Anjelica took his son's hand, and Garrett led his new family home.

The apartment looked brand-new. Not only had his roof been fixed, but there was new carpet. Someone had hung artwork on the walls, framed pictures featuring the American and Texas flags. There were a couple of paintings of mounted Texas Rangers. It actually looked as if someone lived there.

The old sofa was gone and in its place was a large sectional, wide with pillows stacked high and a soft cozy blanket on the back. The old table was still there, but it now had three chairs and a wooden high chair.

Anjelica turned in a slow circle. "Wow. This looks great." She looked at Rio. "Let's go see your and Pilar's room."

Garrett followed, along with both dogs.

After a very brief tour of the new room, they moved to the table.

"They left a macaroni casserole and baked chicken in the oven." She pulled out plates and set the table.

"Pilar, I'm going to put you in the high chair so we can eat." He explained everything step by step as he strapped her into her seat. He made sure to include Rio in his one-sided conversation.

Anjelica handed him a small bowl of cheesy pasta. "Here, feed the baby."

The big brother watched Garrett's every move. "Does your sister eat solid food?"

Rio looked over to Anjelica and nodded. The kid was still refusing to acknowledge him.

She gave him a hesitant smile. "It seems she does."

"Are these safe to give her?" He blew on the hot noodle.

"Does she have teeth?"

Garrett tried to look in her mouth. Sticking his fingers inside didn't seem like a good idea. She smiled at him, showing off a few tiny white teeth. He handed her one curved pasta. Love and adoration radiated from her face. He sat on the chair closest to her and handed her one piece at a time.

"You need to eat, too." Anjelica set a full plate in front of him. She helped Rio into his booster chair.

"I should have thanked them for having this ready for us." Garrett kept his attention on Pilar, making sure she didn't choke.

"They understand that there's times when help is not asked for but needed. Please, don't worry. You thanked them several times, plus you aid the community as a whole. Everyone appreciates your service."

The short silky tail wagged as Bumper sat up on her hind legs. Rio laughed and the little dog jumped up onto his lap.

"Bumper, no. Get down."

Not to be left out, Selena tried to nose her way into Rio's lap, also. The Yorkie jumped onto the table. With a lunge, Selena tried to jump up, but her heavy paws landed on the edge of the plate, flipping it and tossing food through the air.

"Down." Garrett's firm command was instantly obeyed; the dog went to the floor and rolled halfway over, her eyes apologetic. Rio jumped from his chair and covered Selena with his small body.

Garrett's heart twisted. He slowly lowered himself to the floor next to Rio and Selena. With a deep sigh, he placed his hand on Rio's back.

The muscles along the bony spine tensed. "Rio, I'm not going to hit Selena. I just wanted her to sit." Garrett relaxed his jaw.

Anjelica put the little dog in the kitchen and told her to stay. She joined them with a broom in hand and picked up the plate.

He looked at her for help. She offered him a sweet expression of understanding. His attention went back to the boy. "Rio, I'm not mad. I don't want her jumping on the table or begging for food while we eat. It's a bad habit." The Catahoula licked Rio's face. Garrett petted her behind her ears. "She's a good dog. I'm sorry I yelled. Next time I'll make sure to be calm when I give her a command."

Anjelica had scooped some of the food up. "Here, Rio, help me clean. Sometimes accidents happen and we have to take care of the mess."

"She's right. The dogs can learn to stay in a certain area while we eat. Do you think you could teach Selena to mind her manners?"

Rio sat up and nodded. Garrett went to the kitchen and called Selena to him. With her head lowered, she followed.

Anjelica smiled. "It looks as if she's decided to trust your dad." She ruffled Rio's curls.

With a huff, Selena lay on the kitchen mat and watched every movement he made. Bumper sat next to her.

Everyone went back to eating.

Garrett glanced around the table. Family, his family. Time and experience proved he was no family man—he had no clue how to be part of a real family.

What if he let these kids down, like his father had done? Or worse, not take care of them in a world that was unstable. The one time he'd needed to protect a kid, he hadn't been able to. And the result had been devastating. Garrett locked his jaw. He was not going back there, couldn't afford to. That was Afghanistan.

His son needed him. He wouldn't let this kid down, too. He didn't know how, but he was going to be a better father than the man who'd left him.

Kenneth R. Kincaid had taught him one thing: a real father never walked away from the people who were counting on him. Garrett had messed up the first few years of his son's life, but he was here now and nothing was going to get between him and these two kids who needed him. Nothing.

Anjelica gathered the plates off the table.

"So what do we do now?" Sitting between his new son and daughter, Garrett looked as lost as Rio.

"Well, you can have some family time in the living room. Pilar can play on a blanket to build up her strength. I think they would enjoy listening to your music."

"I read online that young kids should be in bed by eight or eight thirty. Then another site said they have internal clocks and know when they need sleep, so a parent shouldn't force a bedtime. What do you think?"

She smiled, biting back the urge to laugh at his uncertain expression. He seemed so vulnerable. "You're the parent. How do you want to set up expectations?"

He picked up Pilar. "Growing up, I didn't have a bedtime."

Pilar closed her eyes and snuggled deeper into Garrett's neck. He rested his cheek against the top of her head. "One of the things I loved about the military was the routine. An eight-thirty bedtime? What about it, Rio?" He laid his hand on top of his son's head.

The little boy crossed his arms and pulled away, looking in the opposite direction.

Her heart twisted at the injured look on Garrett's face. "Eight thirty would be a good time. You'll be fine. All parents struggle trying to figure this out."

Garrett patted the baby's back, his large hands making her look small. "What about baths? She seems too little to put in a tub."

"I could help you give them baths tonight. There's a seat to use in the bath for her. You set up a routine, and they'll start counting on it."

Garrett nodded. "Routines are good. When I'm at work, they'll have the same schedule with you, right?"

"That's the idea." Drying her hands, she turned to face the table. As she leaned against the counter, her heart reeled at the matching expressions on father and son.

Backs straight, they had the same stern look. She knew right then that she was in danger.

"Come on, guys—Rio and Pilar have a new room to explore. Let's go check it out."

They spent the next twenty minutes trying to get him to play in their room. Garrett even read a couple of books with Pilar in his lap as he sat cross-legged on the floor. Oh yeah, she was in trouble.

Falling in love with the children was a risk she was willing to take, but Garrett was not on her list of eligible men. Not only did he risk his life every time he went to work, but he was an alpha male and seemed to be anti-social.

A true loner. He didn't come close to the type of man she wanted to marry. Falling for him would be disastrous to her sanity.

The kids needed her focus. They went through bath time, and with one story, Pilar was sound asleep in her new bed, the crib Anjelica had bought for her daughter. Rio was a little harder, but he snuggled in, and with Selena at the foot of the bed, Garrett and Anjelica eased out of the room.

Whimsical lights danced on the ceiling from the night-light.

They stood in the living room looking at each other. It had been such an eventful day—weekend, actually. Anjelica wasn't sure what to do with this newfound intimacy. Especially with a man who seemed to want none of it—this man she could not, would not love.

Chapter Six

Anjelica walked over to his saxophones. "You did it. Day one in the bag, including dinner, bath and story time."

"Not me, we. Couldn't have done it without you." He wanted to do something for her. Crossing the living space, he went to the freezer. "They stocked my kitchen, including ice cream. I think we deserve a treat."

She joined him in the tiny area. "Sounds like a perfect ending to this day. What can I do to help?"

"Make yourself comfortable on the new sofa. Let me feed you for once. Of course, I'm not actually cooking anything, but it's just as good…almost." He set a bowl on the coffee table in front of her. Neither spoke as they concentrated on eating. Finishing his dessert, he leaned back on a stuffed pillow and savored the silence. The tension he had been holding all day slipped away.

She gathered the bowls and took them to the sink.

"Hey, I'm supposed to do that."

She laughed. "I beat you to it." After washing the simple dishes, she turned to face him. "So what else do you need done? I can stay and talk through anything you're not sure about."

With a grin, he laid his arm across the back of his new sofa. "That would take more hours than we have available. Anyway, you and your Ortega army moved fast. I think your family did everything that needed to be done." He still wasn't sure about all the changes. Was it normal to feel so detached from your own life?

"After seeing those pictures, I had to do something. Your world turned upside down on you. At the same time, duty called, and you had to go out helping others across the county after the storm. The least I could do was make some phone calls. I'm sorry if I overstepped, but we didn't have much time."

"It's as if everything fell into place while I wasn't looking. Thank you." He nodded, not sure what else to say.

"Is there anything else you need?"

He had to snort. That was a loaded question. He didn't know much about kids; there would be things he didn't even know existed. "Not that I can think of for now. I'm a little too wired to go to sleep. I'll play the sax for a while. You can stay if you want."

"That sounds lovely."

With his favorite sax in hand, he went to the balcony. It would soften the noise, and the weather was nice. As his fingers moved over the keys, the music consumed him, releasing the anxiety of the day. *God, thank You for this gift.* He didn't know how to pray. But he could have a conversation with God through notes of his song.

Without it, he was sure he would have lost control of his mental status long ago. As it was, he felt as if a thin string held everything together.

Over an hour had slipped by when he noticed Anjelica standing.

"It's getting late and your little ones will probably be up early. Feel free to call at any time."

He put the sax in its case and followed her to the door. "Thank you. I can't imagine how I would have handled it or gotten any of it done without you."

"God provides before we even know to ask. I'm grateful to help." She reached over and patted his arm.

Her family did that a lot, touched and hugged. For the last three months, he had been trying to avoid her because she would be a complication to his plans. But she ended up being the one to pull everything together and had gotten him through an overwhelming situation. He stepped back before he gave in to the urge to pull her close.

This was not a date. She worked for him. Thoughts of kissing had no business being in his head and needed to be locked down.

She looked so fragile. It just didn't mesh with the warrior she became for his children. A woman who had lost her own child and husband. He had no right to ask more of her.

She smiled one last time, then left, closing the door behind her.

Restless, he put the clean dishes away and went to stand on the balcony. It felt like a lifetime ago that he stood in this exact spot and saw her running through the storm.

Now he needed rescuing. Before heading to the shower, he secured all the doors and windows. Checking on the children, he just stood in the doorway and watched them. They'd probably be up early and he needed to be alert, but sleep seemed dangerous. He hated letting down his guard for any amount of time.

After one of the shortest showers in his life, he

checked on the kids one more time. He couldn't shake the unease that kept his skin tight when the children were out of his sight.

He was going to learn to cope, or he'd never get any sleep and drive them all crazy.

Selena had moved from Rio's bed to the rug in front of the crib. She raised her head and watched as Garrett made his way to see Pilar.

Arms out wide, she was still sound asleep. He petted Selena and turned to check on Rio. The small race-car bed was empty.

His heart jumped to his throat. He couldn't be in the restroom. Had he run away? No, he wouldn't leave Pilar.

Rushing into the living area, he found a chair in front of the pantry and crackers missing. Doing a quick sweep of the apartment, he found all the windows and doors still locked, so Rio had to be in the apartment somewhere. "Rio." He kept his voice low and calm.

Scanning under the beds, he saw just boxes. The first night and he'd lost his son already?

Breathe, Garrett. He's here somewhere. What if he'd hurt himself and couldn't call out? All the horrific scenarios that could happen to a five-year-old flashed through his mind. He shouldn't have left him alone.

He grabbed his phone and hit Anjelica's number. She picked up in one ring. "Garrett, what's wrong?"

"Rio's not in his bed. He took crackers out of the pantry and is hiding somewhere. I can't find him."

"I'm coming up."

He searched the apartment until he heard her at the door. "Thanks." He was saying that a lot lately.

"Not a problem. My guess is that he's close to Pilar."

"That's what I thought, too, but I can't find him."

She got down on the floor. "Rio, come here, *por*

favor." Twisting around, she faced Garrett and pointed under Pilar's crib.

Going to his hands and knees, he scanned the area again, this time slower. That was when he noticed the boxes of diapers had been moved away from the wall.

"What do I do?" Going in and pulling Rio out by his legs didn't seem like the best thing to do to a kid who already had issues.

Selena crawled closer to the edge of the crib next to Anjelica. Her tail thumped against the floor. "Rio, you have a really cool hiding place, but you scared your dad."

Silence. Anjelica reached in and slid a box to the side. There sat Rio, curled up with his superhero blanket.

Garrett got a pillow and comforter from the bed. He joined Anjelica and Selena on the floor. "Hey, little man. If you're going to be sleeping under your sister's crib, you need to make a bed. We also have a food rule I didn't tell you about. If you're hungry, it's okay to get it from the pantry, but you have to eat at the table. No food in the bedroom."

The box of crackers slid out to him. "Okay, thanks. Anjelica is going back to her house for the night. I'll be in the bedroom next door if you need anything."

He looked over at the first woman he had spent any time with since his marriage. "I think he's sleeping there. I used to sleep in my closet. Small spaces can feel safer."

She nodded. "Good night, Rio. Remember, we care about you and need to know where you are when we call your name."

Garrett walked her to the door. "*Thank you* is getting old, but I don't know what else to say."

She laughed. "It works, and it never gets old. I'll

have breakfast ready in the morning, including bacon. See you then."

Once again he closed and locked the door behind her. Standing at the window, he watched until she made it into her house and waited until the lights went out before going to his own bed, where he would toss all night.

Anjelica stood at the kitchen door, cup of coffee in her hand as the sun's early-morning light caressed the landscape. She had fed all her fur babies, gathered the eggs and turned the chickens out. Now a debate battled in her head, pinging back and forth.

Should she go upstairs and help Garrett or wait here? The little ones were Garrett's responsibility, but he had hired her to help. The question was, how much? She knew her family could be a bit forceful in their attempts to help, and she carried the same gene.

During her grief counseling, they'd explored all her weaknesses and strengths, which ironically were the same. Portion control was the key to a happy heart.

What if Garrett was overwhelmed but afraid to ask for help? Taking a sip of coffee, she batted down the urge to run upstairs. It was still early.

The side door of the garage opened and Rio was the first out. He had his hand on Selena's collar. Behind them, Garrett had Pilar wrapped in a blanket. Her heart did a funny flip-flop at the sight of the Texas trooper and his family.

No, no, no. It was a job.

Seeing her at the door, Rio leaped across the sidewalk and ran to her. Garrett looked like he'd gotten even less sleep than she had. And she didn't recall ever seeing him with scruff along his jawline. If she refused to acknowledge his masculine beauty, would it stop enticing the dangerous thoughts that stirred in her brain?

Last swallow of coffee for fortification—then she leaned down to greet Rio.

Garrett gave her a sheepish grin. "We're here. Who knew getting two such small people up and ready would be so complicated."

Hugging Rio, she lifted him as she stood. "I can help in the mornings if you want. That is why I'm here. Once you go back to work, we can set a schedule. With these guys, we need to be ready for a full-court press."

He strapped Pilar into her high chair and headed straight to the coffeepot.

"Not sure I have the energy for a full-court press. I've never needed coffee the way I need it this morning." He actually moaned as the hot liquid slid down his throat.

"I have fresh eggs, bacon and sliced tomatoes. Here, sit down and eat. Do you want orange juice or skim milk?" She offered Rio a small cup of each. He held the mug of milk with both hands like Garrett and took a deep drink, then gave his own little moan. Twinges warmed her heart.

She glanced at Garrett to see his reaction, but he had his head buried in his hands. The timer went off. "How about cinnamon rolls? They were made yesterday."

"I could hang out in your kitchen just for the aromas." He fed Pilar a couple bites of egg before eating the tomato on his plate.

"You know, you hired me to run interference whenever you need it." She gave each of the guys a two-inch-tall cinnamon roll. Licking the gooey goodness off her fingers, she sat down at the table.

"My brain is rubbish this morning, but have you made two sport references in the last two minutes?"

She shrugged and winked at him. "In Clear Water, everyone is a Friday-night-lights fan. Plus I was a total tomboy. I actually had a basketball scholarship but got married instead." Sitting across from him, she grabbed a pear out of the fruit bowl. "Don't let the girlie clothes fool you. On the court, I'm a fierce Mayan warrior. It's the Ortega blood."

Shaking his head, he grinned. "I assumed you were the artsy type that protested violence of any kind."

Changing the subject would be good. "Do you want more bacon?"

"You don't have to feed me. I've managed several years on my own."

"You're not on your own anymore." She nodded and took a bite from the pear.

He cleared his throat. "For some reason, that scares me even more."

Reaching across the table, she touched the back of his hand. "We've got this. You've been given a tremendous gift and it can be consuming, but we'll do this." She glanced at the kids. Pilar played with her eggs and Rio stared at them. It looked as if more of the sugar glaze had gotten on his face and shirt than in his stomach. "We'll set a daily routine and everyone will know what to expect."

Garrett shot straight up in his bed. Breathing as if he had just sprinted two hundred yards. Cries echoed in his head. Swinging his body to the edge of the bed, he planted his feet on the cool surface of the wood floors. Slowing his breathing, he closed his eyes and focused on the present in Clear Water, but the cry came again.

Pilar.

In the next room, Pilar cried. He checked his phone. Three in the morning. In the last two weeks, she had settled into a routine. She was off schedule.

Concerned, he went into the room and found her standing against the railing of the crib, her face red and damp from the tears. Rio was holding a bottle to her, but she slapped it away. The little boy turned and glared at him.

"It's okay, Rio." He crossed the room. She stretched her arms up to him, wanting him to pick her up. Without hesitation, he complied.

Lowering his voice, he started singing "Twinkle, Twinkle, Little Star." With one hand on her bottom, he realized it was a little damp, so he took her to the changing table. "Hey, pretty girl, what's the problem? We're going to get you a fresh diaper, all right?"

Another cry ripped the room as her back arched. This wasn't usual for her. She liked talking and cooing while he changed her.

Rio had pulled up a box and stood at the end of the changing table. He touched her face. It didn't soothe her.

Once she was clean, Garrett lifted her and held her against his shoulder. The soft curls brushed against his stubble as he sang softly against her ear. He'd seen Anjelica do that as she rocked the baby to sleep. Her crying went to a few sniffles and hard hiccups.

Taking a deep breath, Garrett relaxed. He could do this. With another pat on her back, he leaned over the crib to put her back to bed. As soon as he moved her away from him, she started crying again.

Bringing her back to his chest, he started singing. This time it seemed to irritate her. The tiny body stiffened. Rio crossed his arms and glared at him. Even the dog glared.

"It'd help if you could tell me what's wrong. If at least one of you would talk. I can't fix the problem if I don't know what it is." He cradled her in his arms and started swaying. He offered her the bottle again. That didn't help. It seemed to make it worse.

He lifted her back to his shoulder. "You know, when you think of being a father, it's all about playing ball, Christmas mornings and the first bike rides." He massaged her back. His voice low and soft, he walked. "You don't imagine the odd hours or how obsessed you become with the bodily functions of another person."

Pacing back and forth, he tried another song. Maybe he'd done something wrong when he changed her diaper. He laid her down, then took off the onesie and the clean diaper. "Baby girl, I'm trying to fix it." Her skin was smooth, not a mark or blemish.

After what seemed like an hour of Pilar fussing, nodding off, then crying again while Rio and the dog glared at him, he wanted to cry himself. Rio turned his back and marched out the door, Selena on his heels.

"Rio!" A sigh didn't even begin to express his level of frustration as he followed his son.

At the front door, Rio reached up and unlocked it. Okay, he needed to place the lock higher. "It's four in the morning. We are not going outside." The duo headed down the stairs. *Anjelica.* He was going to Anjelica for help.

Okay, so my son is smarter than me. Or maybe the little guy just had better parenting skills.

Whispering soft nonsense words to Pilar, he passed Rio and walked across the driveway to the kitchen door. Pilar's cries had turned to sniffles. "Hang on, baby girl. We're getting help."

Standing in front of the old wood door, he noticed

areas had peeled off, showing years of different paint colors. Pilar nuzzled her nose against his neck. Maybe she had gone back to sleep. He took a step back, about to turn and head back to his living quarters.

Pilar opened her mouth and let out a yell as if he had pinched her. The door opened and Anjelica stood there in an oversize T-shirt and sweats. She glanced down at Rio and Selena, then brought her gaze back to him and Pilar.

"What's up with the family field trip?" She laid a hand on the baby's back.

"I can't settle her down. I've changed her twice, tried to feed her and walked or rocked until… I just don't know what else to do. Rio thought you might be able to help." Okay, so why had he just ratted out his son? "I agreed. So here we are."

She took Pilar. "You and Rio had a conversation about this?"

"Well, no. He walked down the stairs and I followed. Sorry—I know you're not officially on duty, and I hate bothering you, but I don't know what to do to make her all right."

"Have you taken her temp? She feels slightly warm."

He hadn't even thought about her being sick. "No. How do I take her temperature?" He dug his fingers into his hair.

"My aunt left a kit for you that includes an ear thermometer."

"I have to poke something in her ear? That doesn't sound safe."

Pilar reached for him, her lashes wet from tears. "I think she wants you."

"Why? I haven't been able to help her at all." Garrett's hands engulfed her little chubby body. "Should we give her something for the fever?" As he cradled her, she grabbed his thumb and started gnawing on it. Eyes closed, she slobbered all over his hand as her gums went back and forth. "She's trying to eat me."

Anjelica laughed. "I think we might have our answer to what's wrong." Moving around him, she took Rio's hand and headed up the stairs to the apartment. "If she is cutting teeth, it can be painful. Can you feel anything on her gums?"

"But she already has teeth."

"Yes, and she will get more, a whole mouthful."

Pausing, Garrett watch the look of bliss transform the little face as he rubbed a calloused thumb over the swollen gum. "I think I feel something right under the surface." Eyebrows pulled, he looked at her. "How do I fix it so it stops hurting her?"

"Let's take her temp, then go from there, okay?" Anjelica made her way to the nursery and opened the top drawer of the light green dresser. With a weird-looking gun-shaped instrument, she moved to stand in front of him.

Instinctively, he pulled Pilar closer to him. "What are you going to do with that? It looks like it might hurt."

A tiny fist hit Anjelica's thigh. A scowl that mirrored Garrett's was planted on his small face.

"Rio!" Garrett's voice came a little sharper than he intended, causing everyone to jump. Pilar started fussing again. "Shh…baby girl, I'm sorry. It's okay." He turned to his son and took a knee. "I didn't mean to scare you, but you can't hit. You have to use your words."

The small boy reached over and touched his sister's face.

"I want her to be better, too. But I can't allow you

to hit people. In this house, we talk. I promise not to hit Pilar, Anjelica or you. I might yell, but I'll never hit you, and I expect the same from you. We'll fix problems by talking, using our words. Do you understand?"

Rio nodded, then looked up at Anjelica. He licked his lips.

Anjelica dropped to Rio's level also, placing her hand on his shoulder. "Your father asked if this will hurt her. Are you worried about that, too?"

Arms crossed over his middle, he glanced at Garrett.

"Go ahead—use your words."

Thick eyelashes blinked a few times and the only sound in the room was the slurping of Pilar chewing on Garrett's thumb. She fell back to being content in the midst of tension.

"Yes, ma'am."

He spoke! He shot his gaze to Anjelica. *Oh no.* For a moment, Garrett thought Anjelica would start crying. What if that made Rio think he had done something wrong?

He smiled at the boy and patted him on the shoulder. "Good job, Rio."

Anjelica pushed some loose strands of hair back and cleared her throat. "Yes, nice job. I love hearing your voice. Now, about the ear thermometer. What if I show you how it is done? I can use it on your dad first."

Rio shook his head. "Me. Try on me."

"Okay. Ready?" She leaned in closer and showed him the gun, pointing out the details. "I'm going to put it in your ear and push the button. You won't feel a thing." A moment later she showed the screen to Rio. "It says you have a temp of ninety-eight. That's perfect. Now that you know it won't hurt her, let's get Pilar's temp."

Garrett stayed on his knee, with Rio holding Pilar's

hand as Anjelica did her thing. "She has a slight fever. I would hate giving her anything at this point. Let the fever do its job." She looked at Garrett and grinned. "Chewing on you seems to help. I do believe you're the biggest chew toy I've ever seen."

"But how do I get any sleep?" He glanced at the clock. "I have to be at work in four hours."

"We can try some numbing cream for her gums and—" she moved to the basket of toys "—let's see if there's a toy to replace your thumb."

"They make cream for cutting teeth and we have some?"

"Yes, thanks to my family. I'm sure it was Aunt Maggie. She thinks of everything. Since it's so late, or early, depending on how you look at it, let's go ahead and settle them into bed. I'll stay with the kids and you can get a little sleep before going to work, and you won't have to wake them up to bring them to me."

"Are you sure?"

"It's best for everyone."

How would he have survived without her? How had his mother done it all without help? He'd never realized how tired she must have been all the time.

She knew how hard it was to raise two kids alone. One message was the only contact he had had with her in the last two weeks. She was loud and clear about her thoughts of Viviana and told him to let the state take care of them until he knew for sure Rio was his. His mother had never been a fan of his ex-wife.

He stood at the door and watched as Anjelica helped Rio organize the bed he had created under the crib. When she turned and found him staring, she raised her eyebrows.

"Go on with you. We've got this covered, and you

need to get your sleep so I don't have to worry about you tomorrow."

"Yes, ma'am." He needed to leave before he started thinking about her being here permanently and how it felt to be worried over. "Thank you." The words sounded low and rough.

In order to break the invisible chain that held him to the spot, Garrett closed his eyes and spun away from Anjelica and the children.

Creating a fantasy life around a woman had never worked out and now he had a son paying the price. He had one mission and that was to stay focused on Rio and Pilar.

Chapter Seven

The early-morning sun had yet to make an appearance as he pulled into the drive. Today marked one month since Rio and Pilar arrived in his life. House inspections and parenting classes had become the new normal. They were one step closer to official family status.

Before getting the kids from Anjelica, he should go upstairs, lock away his gun and change out of his uniform. He tried to keep his weapons out of Anjelica's sight, knowing how she felt about them, but tonight he needed to see the kids. He needed to touch them and know they were safe before he could go to sleep.

Nothing like an ugly accident on 83 to turn a normal shift into a nightmare. Dealing with death always left him feeling a little hollow.

Home had never looked so good.

Home. Coffee. Sleep.

Maybe he should skip the coffee. In a couple of hours, the kids would be up.

Garrett stifled a yawn as he used his key to open the door into Anjelica's dark house. Normally, he would have left them here and joined them later for breakfast, but there was nothing about tonight. He should have been home hours ago, before their bedtime.

He hoped Anjelica didn't have anything planned for the day. Oh man, he didn't pay her enough. She deserved a big bonus.

Today was officially her day off, but the accident had his shift going seven hours over and he wasn't sure he could function enough to be responsible for the kids.

Easing across the living room, he made sure to side-step a toy truck. He gave a prayer of thanks for his own mother.

There had been so many long hours of two or three jobs, but she had managed to keep them in a safe home with food in the kitchen. He hadn't appreciated her efforts at the time. All he had known was his mom was always gone.

She hadn't had a supernanny like Anjelica or people like the Ortegas to help her when the nights were too long.

He'd call her tomorrow and thank her. She deserved this time to herself and not to be pulled into his drama.

He first checked in Pilar's room and found it empty. His heart jumped and he made sure to control his breathing. All the worst scenarios popped in his head.

The door connecting the nursery to Anjelica's room stood open. With hesitation, he entered, finding it empty, also.

Breathe, Garrett. Breathe. They're here somewhere. He quickly scanned the house and found it empty.

Maybe she had taken them up to the apartment when he had called about being late. He couldn't move fast enough as he leaped the stairs three at a time.

His living room was empty. He rushed to the nursery. A sigh of relief emptied his tense muscles.

All three people of his little family slept safely in the room. Pilar was sprawled on her back with her arms wide, not a care in the world. On the little car bed, Rio lay curled up in Anjelica's lap. She leaned against the wall. They still wore their day clothes.

He smiled at her soft snores. He would have never guessed that she was a snorer—or that he would find it endearing. It made her human.

His family had tried to wait up for him.

Without one of her brightly colored scarves, the soft T-shirt she wore revealed a scar that ran across her collarbone and up her neck. The tip faded into her hairline.

The need to heal Anjelica always lingered, but now it was hard to ignore. She had suffered so much loss and pain. Somehow she still faced life with such openness and willingness to help others.

As gently as possible, he picked up Rio, moving him to the side, and tucked him under his hero blanket. This might be the first time he actually slept in his own bed.

Anjelica shifted to her side and scooted down to the pillow, the soft sounds from her throat stopping. Taking the quilt off the foot of the bed, he covered his pintsize heroine.

She turned her face to him as he tucked the blanket around her. "Garrett, you're home?"

The sleeping edge of her whisper did things to his gut.

"Yes, ma'am." The fresh scent of vanilla and flowers filled his senses. He leaned in closer.

Her hand came up and she threaded her fingers through his hair before they fell to the base of his neck. "Good. We were worried. I listened to the scanner for a bit, but I couldn't…"

His heart expanded in his chest. Emotions that scared

him clogged his throat. "Don't waste your time worrying about me."

Her eyes opened, clouded with sleep. She gave him the softest smile.

He couldn't resist any longer. He leaned forward until his lips pressed against the tiny scar next to her ear. The perfect skin marked with the evidence of the strength she hid under all her softness. He rested there until his breaths synchronized with the pull of her lungs.

Her hand moved back up and smoothed his hair. He wanted to stay there forever. Their pulses dancing to the same rhythm.

Swallowing back the need for real contact, a complete kiss, he forced himself to move and press his lips to her forehead instead. Staring at her, he lingered as long as he dared.

She wanted and deserved a permanent relationship that included a family of her own without mounds of issues.

Pushed past normal limits, his brain cells were not connecting.

Closing his eyes, he stood. She rolled to the other side and tucked her hands under her cheek, snuggling under the quilt.

With slow steps backward, he eased out of the room. As tired as he was, sleep lingered out of his reach. He got a bottle of water, then sat on the sofa.

Anjelica had made it clear from the beginning that she didn't want to get involved with a law enforcer.

He understood her need for security and stability. His job didn't offer either. There were so many guys in his line of work who were divorced, and he was one of them. Restless, he flipped to his side.

A reflection of light caught his attention. The security

light outside had hit the glass of a patriotic poster one of the Ortegas had hung in his apartment. She belonged to a fallen brother and deserved his protection. She needed someone with a safe job and no baggage.

As tired as his body was, his brain wouldn't shut down. He closed his eyes and took slow deep breaths. He needed to go to his own bed, but right now he didn't have the energy to get up.

Down! Down! Cover! He pulled someone's arm to protect them from the explosion.

He had to react faster this time or they were going to die.

"Garrett." Soft fingers pressed against his jaw.

He opened his eyes and found his hand gripping Anjelica's wrist. Hard. She lay next to the sofa awkwardly.

He let go and jumped to his feet. Holding his hand out to help her up, he tried to stop shaking. Or at least hide it. *Five...four...three. Breathe.*

"I'm so sorry." He scanned her for any injuries, not able to bring himself to look her in the eye.

She took his hand and rose up in front of him. "I'm not hurt. You were trying to protect me. You said, 'I got you. I got you.' You pulled me down as if to shield me." Cupping her hand around his jaw, she forced his face toward her. "Really, you weren't trying to hurt me." Stepping closer, she put both hands on his face and made him look at her, in the eye. "Next time I'll be more careful when I wake you up."

"You shouldn't have to be careful." He moved out of her reach.

"Garrett." She used the voice she used when Rio was

upset. "You lived in and survived a war zone. I would have to be clueless to not be aware of PTSD."

"I've been home for over five years. I don't have PTSD. It was just a bad dream."

"Have you talked to someone about these bad dreams? Do they happen often? Maybe Jake can help you. He was a marine and—"

"I don't need to talk to anyone. Now you sound like Torres. This is the problem living with people. They want to know all your business and ask questions."

"You've talked about this with Jake?"

"No."

She sighed, a deep heavy one of frustration. "I'm only asking because I care about those kids in the next room." She crossed her arms and glared at him, the sweet concerned expression gone.

Blood left his face and limbs. "What if it had been Rio? Or what if he saw me pulling you to the ground? It would've terrified him to see me attack you like that." He had become a danger to the ones he should be protecting.

"Garrett, it's all good. You didn't attack me. Rio is fine." She moved toward him with her hand out. He did a side step around the sofa. "I need to go for a run." He looked back to the door to the room where she and the kids slept last night. He needed to get out of the house, to push his physical limits in order to get out of his own head. "Can you watch the kids for a little bit longer?"

"Of course I'll watch the kids. You've had less than two hours of sleep. So take your run, take a shower, then get some real sleep. We'll be fine. I have some shopping to do in Uvalde—I'll take the kids with me. It's good for them to get out of the house. Later today the family's coming over to make piñatas and confetti eggs, *cascarones*, for Easter. We'll be outside. So you can stay in your room and sleep."

"Easter? Isn't it a little early?"

"With my family's crazy schedule? No this is the only time we can all get together, and it's a big family event. We don't want anyone left out."

He nodded like he understood while keeping the sofa between them. His eyes went to the scarf she had on, but he knew how soft she was under the bright blue material. Kissing her on the scar had been a huge mistake. Now he had a hard time getting the thought of a real kiss out of his head. He really needed that run.

With Garrett stalking out of the room, Anjelica flopped back on the sofa. She picked up the pillow Garrett had been using when she went to wake him up. From the kids' room, she'd heard Garrett having a nightmare. Her plan had been to wake him up and tell him to go to bed while she stayed and made breakfast.

The pillow in her lap smelled like the soap he used. With a heavy sigh, she stood. Rio and Pilar would be getting up soon. She needed to get them fed and out of the apartment by the time Garrett finished his run. He probably needed sleep. He also needed to talk to someone, but that was out of her control.

Later she'd do some research on PTSD. It seemed they were living with two males who had an overzealous need to protect the people in their lives.

Garrett needed psychotherapy as much as his son did. Maybe he hadn't been suffering from PTSD, but with the upheaval in his life, it might have kicked in for the first time or returned. She needed to find out if that was possible.

As she started working in the kitchen, Garrett came

out with his Marines T-shirt and sweats. Selena sat still as he put on her leash.

He gave her a sheepish grin. "Are you sure it's all right if I go for a run? I can keep it short."

"No. Go for as long as you need. I'm going to make breakfast. If we're gone when you get back, I'll leave you a plate in the oven."

"Thanks, you don't ha—"

Her stare stopped him cold. "Don't you dare say what I think you are about to say. I don't do anything I don't want to do. We'll be in Uvalde most of the day. Even when my family gets here, you can ignore them. I'll explain you were at the accident site all night. They'll understand. Of course, anytime you want to, you can join us."

"Okay." Walking past her, he leaned in and gave her a light kiss.

They both jumped back as if reacting to an electrical shock. Her heart lodged in her throat. She blinked. It hadn't been a dream. Last night he had kissed her.

Not a normal kiss, but next to her ear. He had kissed the edge of her scar. Her hand pressed against the spot, heat radiating from her skin. His gaze darted around the room. "I'm sorry. I just…"

Anjelica couldn't read the emotions on his face. He turned toward the front room, then back to her.

He ran his fingers through his hair, leaving it standing in the cutest way. A very dangerous adorable helpless look settled on his face.

"It's okay, Garrett. Go for your run."

With a nod, he was gone.

Standing alone at the screen door, she touched her fingers to her lips.

Chapter Eight

Garrett flipped onto his back. Interlocking his fingers over his chest, he lay still and focused on the sounds of Anjelica's family having fun. If he strained, he could hear talking and laughing with music in the background. A few times kids' voices erupted in squeals, only to fade away quickly.

He worried about Rio wanting to hide instead of running and laughing with the other children. Maybe he should go check on him.

Anjelica would be there, and after last night—and then the accidental kiss this morning—he didn't know what to say to her.

To get his mind off his emotional battles, he imagined Pilar having a great time being passed around while Rio hovered and stressed over all the strange people. Music came through the walls, not from speakers but live strings and a trumpet.

He stood and walked to the balcony. Pulling the heavy drapes back, he saw a yard full of color, people, animals and tables. The big garden in the middle of it all had started to turn green. As he scanned the area, the size of the crowd surprised him. A group of men had guitars, basses and the trumpet he heard. Anjelica ran over and talked to them. Her hands flew as the yellow scarf she wore fluttered around her, tangled in her dark hair.

Glancing at the clock, he calculated he had slept eight hours straight without interruptions. That was the longest stretch of sleep he'd had since becoming a father.

After a quick wash and shave, he changed and headed to the door. But before his hand touched the knob, there came a faint knock. The hinges creaked as it slowly opened. Rio poked his head in the small opening.

Garrett crouched down. Rio's eyes widened before he gave his dad a tentative smile.

"Hey, little man. Everything all right?"

Rio nodded, his curls falling into his eyes. His small hand pushed his hair back, allowing him to scan the room. Garrett froze midaction as he realized he was making the exact same gesture. "Were you looking for me?"

Another small nod. Then he looked down at his shoes.

"Rio, you have to use your words. This is a safe place to talk." He refrained from reaching out to stroke the boy's hair. This was the first time his son sought him out. He didn't want to do anything to startle him. Slowing his breathing, he held still and waited.

"Anjelica said you were sleeping." Rio rubbed his thumb against his palm. "Are you awake now?"

A lightness lifted the corners of his mouth. "Yeah, I'm awake. Thank you for letting me sleep and coming to check on me." He wanted to reach out and hug his son.

"Rio?" Anjelica's voice drifted from the bottom of the stairs. "Your dad is sleeping."

Standing, Garrett opened the door all the way. "I was up and about to come out when Rio came in to check on me." He gently squeezed the little shoulder. "We were just talking."

Anjelica's eyes widened a bit before she gave him an understanding look. "Well, as long as everyone's good, I'll head back to the party. We've dried the eggs for the *cascarones* and are stuffing them with confetti. Then we'll start adding the paper and glue to the piñatas." She clasped her hands in front of her waist. "So does this mean father and son will be joining the festivities?"

"Come on, son, let's go make a piñata." Okay, that was not something he'd ever dreamed of saying, but it felt right.

As they stepped through the back door of the garage, most of the crowd stopped and stared at them. Rio ducked behind his legs.

Anjelica clapped. "Now that Garrett's awake, we don't have to stay quiet. Tío Guillermo, you can start the music again." She laughed as children of all ages dashed to the table she had covered in large canvas sheets. "I'll be at the piñata table. Join me when you're ready."

Celeste, just a year or so older than Rio, ran over to his son. "Hey, Rio, I was looking for you. Do you want to come help make the piñata? It's really messy and fun."

Rio blinked at Pastor John's daughter a few times but didn't make an effort to move away from Garrett. "Rio doesn't talk much."

She smiled at him, then back at Rio. "That's okay. Daddy says I talk enough for a whole pack of people." She held out her hand. "You don't have to talk if you don't wanna."

Eyes so much like his own looked up at him. Garrett went to his knee. "Do you want me to go with you?"

Rio nodded and slipped his hand into Garrett's as the little high-energy blonde grasped the other and started skipping to the table. "You'll love it. We make two, a giant one for the bigger kids and a smaller one for, well, the smaller kids." She laughed as she looked back at Rio. His son just nodded and watched her in complete fascination.

Maybe being led around by pretty girls started early for the Kincaid males.

On the table, two bamboo-framed structures were being covered in strips of newspaper and white paste. It looked messy. Adults and kids laughed as they criss-crossed the strips. Glue covered everything. Rio looked up at Garrett, doubt in his expression.

Garrett sighed. He had his own doubts about this adventure. Celeste laughed and pulled Rio into the middle of the crowd. People shifted and gave them room.

The enthusiastic daughter of the pastor plunged her hands into the bucket full of the glue mix, then pointed to a stack of torn paper. "Rio, hand me the paper and I'll coat it in glue. Then we can put them on the donkey. It's the donkey that carried Jesus into town before he was arrested."

Doing what he was told, Rio glanced up at him with a bit of panic in his eyes. Garrett came in close to him. "Do you know the Easter story of Jesus?"

He shook his head. Celeste gasped. "I thought everyone knew the Easter story." On her knees, she twisted around and yelled, "Daddy!"

Rio turned the opposite direction as if looking for an escape route. Picking him up, Garrett placed him on his lap. "It's okay. Not everyone knows the story."

Pastor John came over carrying the guitar he had been playing. "What's wrong, Celeste?"

"He doesn't know about the donkey that carried Jesus or the Crucifixion or the Resurrection. Can you tell him the story of Jesus and Easter?"

Some other people came over and Pastor John pulled up a chair to the end of the table. "My favorite story to tell from the Bible is the Resurrection of Jesus. Rio, do you want to hear it?"

With a nod, he started scanning the crowd. Garrett assumed he searched for Anjelica. She had Pilar and was walking across the yard, heading straight to the table, which had collected a crowd. Garrett made sure to sit still, not fidget or scan the crowd for threats. This was a happy family event.

One of the older kids complained about it not being Easter yet, so why did they have to hear the story again?

Anjelica stopped to stand next to them. "I would love to hear the story, Pastor John. It's a story we should hear often all through the year. I even have some Resurrection eggs. Rio can show everyone as you tell it." She handed Pilar to him.

Garrett settled her on one leg as he balanced Rio on the other. "It's been a long time since I heard the story. Pilar's never heard it, either."

A few others joined them at the table. With a couple of strums of his strings, Pastor John's soothing voice started recounting the days that led up to the ultimate sacrifice.

Anjelica handed an egg to Rio at each turn of the story. He carefully looked inside to discover something that had to do with the journey. The other men who had been playing now gave the story a soft musical background.

Garrett had never been so moved. He sat with his children and listened to the story of how he'd gained the undeserved path to forgiveness. This was the reason he'd given up life as a solitary bachelor. These moments made every sacrifice worth it.

"Why did he do it?" Rio whispered, surprising everyone who had never heard him speak. Garrett had no clue how to respond.

Pastor John set the guitar down and leaned forward. "That's a great question. The Bible tells us that God so loved the world that He gave His only son. He loved us so much He didn't want to be separated from us. We are His children and He wants to be with us forever, even past this life."

Rio's expression turned even more serious as he processed the new information. He had to have questions about his mom and the way she died.

Celeste handed Rio a strip of newspaper. "My mommy's in heaven like yours." Rio scooted off Garrett's leg and stood closer to Celeste in order to smear the glue-coated paper over the soon-to-be Easter donkey.

Needing to stretch his legs, Garrett stood. He made a face at his daughter. Pilar laughed and grabbed his nose. A sunny yellow headband gathered her dark curls away from her face. He realized he would have no idea how to fix her hair if he was alone. Something else for his ever-growing list of things he'd thought he would never need to know.

As she made sounds, he talked back to her. She had to be the happiest baby ever.

In the early years, Viviana planned and dreamed about the kids they would have one day, a boy and a girl. "If your mamma was here, she'd play with you and love you." He lifted her up and rubbed her tummy with his nose. The giggles would cure anyone's sour mood. His own smile felt good as he continued to play with her.

"She's looking so much healthier since you brought her home." Buela stood next to him, wiping her hands on her green-and-pink apron. "Can I hold this precious girl? Anjelica is looking for you."

His daughter laughed and reached for the tiny grandmother.

"Where is she?" He scanned the backyard, which had turned into an impromptu fiesta. Kids played chase with the baby goats around the outside of the garden.

Next to the yellow blooming Esperanza with a small group of women stood one of the most beautiful women he had ever met. Anjelica threw her head back. A hearty laugh with no apologies consumed her whole body.

Her face lit up when he joined the group. "Garrett, I was just telling them that you play several instruments."

"She said you played in the military band." An older man spoke, one of Anjelica's uncles, but Garrett couldn't remember which one. "Why don't you join us?"

That was all it took. Before he knew what happened, Garrett was playing with them and being invited by Pastor John to join the church band. Music had always been the thing that grounded him.

It was another gift God had given him that he took for granted. What had he done to deserve all the gifts that now made his life worth living? Rio, Pilar and Anjelica.

Maybe he should give something back. One thing his mom taught him was to always be grateful when others did something kind for you. She made sure he showed his appreciation.

He didn't have much to offer, but he had his music. His music was about the only thing worth giving.

Anjelica turned her face into the gentle breeze that wove its way through the backyard. It danced with the trees, adding its own music to the gathering. Rio sat in her lap as he watched his sister. Pilar played on the blanket next to the Esperanza that Garrett had helped her save. She played with Rio's soft curls. Her daughter would have been just a little younger than Rio. She bit the inside of her cheek.

Pilar laughed and threw one of her teething toys. So much stronger than a month ago, and she had a smile for everyone. Rio, not so much, but at least he was not scowling at everyone who walked by. Just the ones who talked to him.

The brightly colored piñatas were hanging in the tree drying, and the hollowed-out eggs were filled with confetti. Now everyone sat around listening to the music her uncles, Pastor John and Garrett played.

This was living. She closed her eyes and thanked God for His many blessings. She couldn't resist kissing Garrett's son on the top of his head. He turned and looked at her.

"I was just thanking God for the perfect day with so many people that love each other. Look how strong Pilar is getting. She pulled herself up to sit."

Celeste sat on the edge of the baby blanket and started talking to her. Rio eased down from Anjelica's lap and sat next to his sister. Anjelica wasn't sure if he was being protective or saw Celeste as a new friend.

Glancing over at Garrett, she saw that he was watching, too. They made eye contact and he raised his eyebrow in question. Shrugging, she gave him a smile and sat back. Watching him play was pure pleasure.

Her grandmother joined her. "Something about a man playing music just stirs your heart, doesn't it, *mija*? I saw your *buelito* play at a friend's party and I fell in love."

"Buela, please don't start."

"You need to open your heart or the years will slip by and you'll be alone."

"Being alone is not the end of the world. The wrong man would make it worse. I'd rather be alone than miserable."

"Oh, *mija*, he's a good man."

The only way to get out of this argument was to stop talking. Eyes closed, Garrett had lost himself in his music. Why couldn't he be an auto mechanic or a banker who played the saxophone? Why did he have to make a living by putting himself in direct danger?

Behind the garden, her brothers had started a bonfire with the pruned limbs from her pecan trees. She loved the smell of pecan wood burning. Soon it would be too hot and dry to light a fire.

Her grandmother was right about her heart wanting to love again. Her wayward thoughts of Mr. Hero Man apparently proved she was ready to try a new relationship. Maybe she should join a singles' group in Kerrville.

There was no way she was going to hand her heart over to another save-the-world kind of man. She sighed. Pilar pulled at Rio's hair. The children laughed.

These two already had her heart, but she had to draw the line at their father.

She glanced at the object of her denial. His eyes were closed as he absorbed the music. She had to figure something out because she knew, without a doubt, she was already walking across dangerous ground.

"Tía Anjelica, there's a man at the door that's looking for Officer Kincaid." Her nephew Jordan looked concerned. "He looks official. He's in a suit." He glanced at her charges on the blanket, then leaned in close to her. "I think he might be here about the kids."

She patted him on the back. "It's okay. Will you watch the children for me while I see what he wants?" She tried to tell herself there was no reason to worry. It was late Saturday. Maybe they were just his last visit for the day.

"Thank you, Jordan. I'll be right back."

"Yes, ma'am." The lanky teen plopped down next to the blanket.

Should she get Garrett or see who it was first?

Before she could decide, Garrett had noticed her standing and staring at him. He raised an eyebrow in question. She gave him a slight nod. Without hesitation, he put down the sax and walked over to her.

"What is it? Is something wrong?" He turned from her and scanned the yard.

"There's a visitor at the front door. No one I know uses the front door. A man in a suit. It might not be CPS, and I was debating if I should tell you now or after I knew for sure."

"We knew he could be stopping by to see how the kids were doing." He smiled. "This is good. Look at Pilar sitting up. Rio is hanging with other people without a blanket over his head, and he's started talking to us. I think this is good timing."

"You're right. Not sure why I feel all jittery." As she turned to go into the house, Garrett followed, placing his hand on the small of her back. She relaxed. *"Si Dios quiere."* We will trust in God's will.

"Si Dios quiere," he repeated in his Texas drawl. The warmth of his breath tickled her neck as he leaned in close to her ear. The solid weight of his touch created a warm, safe feeling. She hurried ahead through the kitchen, forcing him to drop his hand.

She clenched her fist. His touch was no different than that of her father or brothers. No different, no different.

For her next day off, she was determined to look into the singles' group at the church in Kerrville. A teacher would be nice. She could date a teacher.

"Officer Kincaid. Mrs. Ortega-Garza. How are you doing?" John Ackerman held out his hand to Garrett, then her.

"We're good. Is this an official visit? Was there another house inspection that needed to be done?" Garrett smiled at the man, looking completely at ease.

She remembered her manners and greeted the man, too. "Nice to see you again. Would you like something to drink or eat?"

A shake of his head had her jumping ahead to why he might be here. "The kids are doing great. Pilar is sitting up and Rio has started talking to Garrett. Both of them are outside with my family. They're so happy." *Breathe. Anjelica, breathe.* Garrett reached over and took her hand. She didn't look at him. She couldn't.

"That sounds great, but I'm actually here to give you some bad news. Well, maybe you'll like it. I know the placement was an emergency and you had not been aware of your son."

Now he squeezed her hand a little tight. "But he's mine now, right? Both are doing well here. Is there a problem?"

"Are you still wanting to adopt the girl?"

"Pilar." Garrett nodded.

She realized she had stopped breathing. With a deep breath, she relaxed her muscles and tried to calm her rolling stomach.

"The paternal grandmother has changed her mind and has petitioned the courts for full guardianship. So if you had doubts about taking a child that's not your biological daughter, then this is good. But if you're serious about being a parent to both? Well, not so good."

Garrett's fingers tightened, then relaxed around her hand. He repeated the motion, but when she looked at his face, he seemed unfazed by the news.

"What are her chances of getting custody? Since I'm his father, they can't take Rio from me." His gaze stayed focused on the CPS worker.

"No, no. Rio's yours. Do you want to fight for custody of the girl?"

He glanced at her. The panic buried in the depth of his eyes tore her heart.

She returned the grip on his hand before turning to Mr. Ackerman. "But the court would want to keep the kids together, right? I don't understand—we were led to believe there was no one that wanted Pilar."

Mr. Ackerman pushed his glasses up and nodded. "When we arrived on the scene, they were our first contacts. At the time, they made it clear they didn't want the children. Now that things have settled, Cecilia Barrow, the deceased father's mother, claims to have changed her mind."

Garrett stepped away with a low growl. "Viviana would have wanted me to have both of them. They need to stay together." He ran his fingers through his hair before turning back to them, his stone face back in place. "What do I need to do to secure Pilar as my daughter?"

"Well, go forward with your petition, stating that you want to keep your son and his sister together. The kids have an appointed lawyer. But the final decisions will be with the judge. She tends to go with blood, but for this case, that's hard. On one hand her brother, on the other her grandmother. There's just no way of knowing." He looked around the house. "How are the children settling?"

Anjelica jumped in before Garrett could say anything. "Rio still prefers sleeping close to his sister. They're very close, and the doctor that Rio is seeing says that it will help him if he can choose where to sleep. It gives him some control in a limited way."

Mr. Ackerman smiled and nodded. "Yes, I'm aware of the recommendations."

"Oh. Okay. Do you want to see the kids? They really are thriving here with Garrett." She needed to stop talking.

"That sounds great."

Planting a sweet smile on her face, she led them through the house. The three of them stopped on the porch.

"This is a great house. Do you plan to stay long-term, Officer Kincaid?"

"Call me Garrett. The kids are by the garden." He went stiff. It was subtle, but she saw the shift in his stance. He was on guard.

She scanned the yard to see what had upset him. Her family was in different groups, most split between the music and building up the bonfire. A few were playing horseshoes. She glanced to her yellow-flowered bush.

She stopped breathing. They were gone. Celeste, Rio

and Pilar were not on the blanket. Even the blanket had vanished. They had to be around somewhere.

She looked for Jordan. He had joined the group at the fire pit. Oh no. The fire was dancing about four feet into the air. Where were the kids?

Chapter Nine

A buzz vibrated Garrett's skull. The popping of the burning wood amplified across the yard. Something in the corner of his eyesight flashed. He cleared the steps and was in front of Jordan before a complete thought formed in his head. The teen had been in charge of his missing children. A dog barked.

The pressure on his chest tightened. He needed to say something to Jordan, but he couldn't speak. An explosion went off and he turned, ready to dive in and get the kids out.

He had lost the kids. Sounds and movements blurred. He tried to focus on his hands. They were shaking.

He was in Anjelica's backyard. A warm body brushed against his leg as a cool nose pressed against his hand. Cool nose? He looked down and saw Selena, her one blue eye and one brown eye looking up at him. If she was here, the kids were close. They were okay.

Jordan took a step back.

"Garrett?" A hand touched his arm.

Taking a deep breath, he forced each muscle to release the tension. To lose control now would be the worst timing. Half the community stood around watching, along with the caseworker.

His hand dug into the soft coat of the big cattle dog, and he made a point to look Anjelica in the eyes. He needed an anchor and he needed it fast. He'd be useless to the kids if he wasted time battling phantom enemies from the past.

She leaned in close. "Garrett, they're inside the garden. Under my beanpoles."

The edge of Rio's favorite blanket poked out from under the wooden pole structure built for the bean vines. It was in the shape of a tepee.

Jordan's gaze darted between Garrett and the kids. "Oh, *Tía*, I'm sorry. They were just playing. Celeste and Rio were pulling her around on the blanket. I thought they'd be fine. I didn't realize…"

Garrett nodded and moved that way. He had to get his children. Rio had gone into his hiding mode again. Which meant he was frightened.

As they got closer, he heard sweet giggling. For the first time since he noticed them missing, he breathed.

Don't let them see you upset. The CPS worker was right behind him. He could *not* show any weaknesses, not with his guardianship of Pilar at risk.

If they thought he was unstable in any way, they might take Rio, too.

Selena barked and ran to the garden gate. She sat next to the poles. Getting as close to the kids as she could, she looked back at Garrett, her big tail thumping the ground.

A miniature goat with long gray hair and a black face had gotten into the garden and climbed the steep edge of the slanted poles. Head down, ready to butt anyone who got close to the kids.

Anjelica gathered the goat into her arms. Going down on her heels, she peeked under the superhero tent.

"Hey, guys, you worried us." The corner of the blanket was pulled out of her hand. At the same time Celeste popped up from the other side, laughing.

"Rio took Pilar for a ride on her blanket. She laughed the whole way. This is the coolest garden and it's not even full of plants yet." She looked under the blanket, than back to Anjelica and Garrett. "Did we do something wrong? We were just playing."

"Sweetheart, you can't take a baby for a ride away from the adults."

"But they can still see us. Daddy says not to get out of eyesight." Her smile was gone. "Oh, that's the rule for me because I'm a big girl. I guess a baby has to stay put. I'm sorry."

Garrett moved to the other side of the structure and got down to Rio's level. Not that the boy would notice. He had his head tucked down and knees pulled up. He couldn't have made himself any smaller. Pilar looked at him and smiled when Garrett reached to pull her into his arms. "Rio, I'm going to give Pilar to Anjelica."

His son had his hand on his sister's arm. He tried to pull her closer.

As gently as he could, Garrett removed Rio's death grip and lifted the baby off the ground. Tucking her into his arms, he touched her tiny chin and smiled at her. "Your big brother took you for a ride?" His heart was in a knot. Now the grandmother wanted to take Pilar from them.

Her son had killed Viviana. The woman had turned her back on them and now wanted to claim her. It wasn't right. Everything tilted out of control.

He glanced at the CPS worker. The man observed

every move they made, every word that was spoken. Had he noticed how close to the edge Garrett was when he found the children missing?

Anjelica moved in next to him. "Here, let me take her and you talk to Rio. I think both of us leaving his sight with all of the people, and then the caseworker showing up, was too much for him."

Garrett nodded. "You're right. One of us should have stayed with him and explained what was going on." He handed over Pilar. He moved closer and, in a low voice, whispered in Anjelica's ear, "What do we say about the grandmother?"

She peeked down at Pilar, then gave him a half-hearted smile. "I wish I knew. Let's just get him calm and in the house. Then we'll deal with what we tell him."

Warm fingertips touched his face. He wanted to capture her warmth. He was proud of himself for not grabbing her hand and pressing it against his lips. How had life gotten so complicated that he needed his crazy landlady to save him?

"I'll tell my mom that we have to deal with the children's case. She'll take care of everyone here. If I take Pilar inside, I'm pretty sure you can get your little man to follow without a fuss." Her hand went back to tending the baby.

What would she do if he leaned in and kissed her? Her deep golden eyes darted away from him, glancing over his shoulder. Ugh, Mr. Ackerman watched.

Garrett stepped back and nodded. "Go ahead and talk to your mom. Rio and I will meet you and Pilar in the house." He made sure to say it loud enough for Rio to hear. "Celeste, you go with Ms. Anjelica."

"Yes, sir. Sorry about taking the baby for a ride."

The woman who was becoming indispensable to him and his family walked away. He wanted to call her back, to run after her. She stopped and spoke briefly with Mr. Ackerman.

The heavy weight on Garrett's shoulders stayed in place as he dropped to the ground. After waiting for a bit, he picked up the corner of the superhero blanket. Rio had his head up.

"Your sister's fine. She's in the house with Anjelica. I plan on joining them as soon as you're ready. I'm not going to leave you, Rio. Even if you can't see me, I'm here."

The boy wiped at his face and glanced at Garrett. "He's not taking us away?"

Garrett's gut twisted. "No, little man, you're mine. No one is taking you away from me."

"What about Pilar?" He scooted closer to Garrett. The edge of the blanket fell away.

How much should he tell him without causing more damage? "Pilar does have a grandmother that wants to see her. Do you know Cecilia Barrow?"

He nodded. "Grandma CeCe. She was nice." He had scooted all the way over to Garrett and wedged himself next to his leg. A couple of the small goats had wandered back into the garden, nosing around. They looked exhausted from all the running earlier. The white one made himself comfortable next to Garrett. Rio gave a soft giggle as the gray one started chewing on his ear or hair. Garrett couldn't figure out which, but he was pretty sure he needed to stop it.

Garrett had to smile. How had he found himself sitting in a country garden with a son and a goat on either side of him?

"So, little man, are you ready to go inside? I promise

I'll tell you if anything is going to change for our family." He brushed back the one dark curl that flopped over Rio's eye. "That's what we are now. I didn't know you were with your mom, but now I have you and I'm not going to let anyone hurt you. You also have to tell me if you're worried or scared. Together we'll fix it. You're not alone, Rio. Do you understand?"

With a sigh carrying a hundred years of burdens, his son stood. He might be five, but he had the eyes of an old war-weary vet.

Garrett stood, dusting off his pants. With one hand he picked up the discarded blankets, and the other he held out for Rio to take. "Let's put these goats up before they eat Ms. Anjelica's new plants."

The small fingers reached for his as they put the goats up for the night. He swung Rio up, and they made their way across the yard full of people and into the house, where Mr. Ackerman waited. Garrett had to find a way to keep his family together.

Anjelica imagined Garrett wanted to hide from the world tonight. Mr. Ackerman had finished his inspection and told them everything he knew of the grandmother's claim. After he left, she and Rio had joined the family for a while and watched the bonfire burn down. Garrett sat on the porch swing holding Pilar, wrapped in a blanket.

As Anjelica climbed the steps, he opened the blanket and invited her to hide with them. Rio sat with Celeste, roasting marshmallows as her family sang songs. Settling in next to father and daughter, she bowed her head for a small prayer. *Lord, these babies deserve a place of love and peace to heal their wounds. Please let it be here, if that is Your will.*

Her heart and mind could not imagine anyone taking Pilar from her family, from Garrett.

Family by family, everyone left. Now the four of them unwound from the day's hectic activity and bad news in her art studio while Garrett played soft jazz.

As his fingers played random melodies that relaxed them, her hands shaped the wet clay as it spun on the wheel. Anjelica blocked out all the worries and focused on shaping a new vase. The sweet sounds of Garrett's saxophone floated around the room as he stood in the open doorway. Rio had his own slab of clay, and Pilar bounced in her colorful bouncer.

She stopped the pottery wheel and looked at the round wide bowl her vase had turned into.

Rio yawned as he formed what looked like a bear. Gently setting his sax to the side, Garrett smiled at his son.

"I'm not finished making Selena. I want to make Bumper, too."

"I'll put them in a plastic bag for you so you can work on them later."

Anjelica wanted to wrap all three of them in love and make the real world go away, just like they had under the family quilt. She had no power over what happened outside this home, or even the hurt and doubt inside Garrett's heart. No matter how much she wanted to.

Instead she gave him her best smile. "Can we play a little longer? They can stay here tonight. We can camp out in the playroom."

Rio's eyes went wide and he nodded. "Please."

With his troubled eyes, Garrett forced a smile. "Sounds like a plan." He lifted Pilar and she snuggled into his neck.

Anjelica worried that he didn't get enough sleep.

The landline rang. Her heart jumped. She'd forgotten about that phone. It never rang. "The answering machine'll pick it up. If it's important, I'll call back. Probably a sales call."

"Hey! Anj. It's me, Jewel. You didn't answer your cell and we need to talk." The voice on the machine belonged to one of her middle sisters. "Call me back when you get a chance. I have a gift for you." Laughter bounced out of the phone. "You are going to love me more than you do now."

Before the voice cut off, a knock on the door startled her. She glanced at Garrett. "Okay, this is getting weird. No one ever comes out here except for family." She was grateful he was here. "And they never knock. It's too late for the UPS man, and CPS has already been here."

With a nod, Garrett stood, putting his hand on the place he normally wore his gun. He shook his head and winked. "I'm sure it's fine. Stay here with the kids and I'll check it out." He turned to the dogs. "Stay."

Selena sat up straight next to Rio and watched as Garrett walked through the door. Bumper ignored the command and ran for the front door.

The barking got louder and faster before Anjelica heard the door open. Then there was a high-pitched "Coco!" followed by silence.

She heard another deep male voice join Garrett's.

"Anjelica." Garrett came to the door. "They say that they're here for their dog. Appears Bumper's real name is Coco."

Now? It had been over a month. She had started to think of Bumper as hers. Rio moved to stand next to her. With a tight smile, she took his hand and headed to meet Bumper's family.

Picking up Pilar, she stepped into the living room

to find a red-haired little boy rolling on the floor with an overly excited Bumper. The little boy had the most electric-blue eyes she had ever seen.

A man kneeled next to them. He looked up at her and stood, holding out his hand. Now she had seen that shade of blue twice. The young boy had to be his son.

"Hello, I'm Dane Valdez, the new athletic director at Clear Water ISD. I met your sister at Garner State Park. She told me you had found Coco. Sorry it's so late. I had planned to come tomorrow after church, but Alex was too excited to get her back, he talked me into coming tonight." He gave them an embarrassed grin. "We thought we lost her in Dallas, but she must have slipped out of her crate when we were looking at houses last month."

The boy was now sitting up and the little dog was licking his face. "Daddy, I told you we'd find her. We can take her to our new home."

Garrett looked behind her. "Where's Rio?" He moved to the doorway. "Rio?" He looked back at her, concern in his eyes. "I don't see him or Selena."

"He was just with me."

Coach Valdez looked at her. "Does your son hide often? Alex went through a hiding phase."

"Oh, I'm the nanny. Garrett's their father."

Garrett's jaw flexed. "What if he ran—"

She didn't give him time to finish. Putting Pilar in his arms stopped him. "Here, take her. I have an idea where he's gone." She headed to the kitchen.

Garrett turned to the stranger in their house. "It's been a rough day." He gently bounced Pilar as she started fussing. "Shh. It's okay, baby girl." He followed Anjelica to the kitchen.

The father and son were close behind him.

"What's a nanny?" the boy asked his father.

"Someone that helps take care of kids in their house when the parents are working." The new coach put a hand in his pocket. "Have we come at a bad time? Jewel said she would call you and let you know." He put his free hand on his son's shoulder. "We can leave. I'll call about Coco tomorrow."

"Daddy, no! I want to take Coco home now."

Anjelica found Rio in the washroom, trying to get into the dryer for his blanket, which was almost done drying. "Rio, it's okay. Bumper is their dog and they're very happy to find her."

Rio turned and looped his arms around Selena, burying his face in her fur.

Anjelica went to her knees. "Sweetheart, they aren't taking Selena. She's yours, but Coco was just here waiting—" her throat starting burning; she could cry later, not now, not in front of Rio "—for her family to come get her. Just like your dad came and got you."

She looked out into the kitchen and smiled at Garrett's stern face. "He tried to get his blanket so he could hide Selena."

The little boy holding Bumper...Coco...stepped closer. "Rio? That's a cool name. I'm sorry we scared you. My mom gave me Coco before she died. I had promised to take care of her, but she runs away a lot. Thank you for taking care of her."

Rio walked out of the washroom, his hand tight around Selena's collar. He looked at the boy, who was a few years older than him. With several slow steps, he stood in front of Alex and patted the silky mop of a dog. "My mom gave me Selena, too. She is named after a famous singer my dad likes."

"Is your mom dead, too?"

Rio nodded.

Anjelica swallowed. "So you're moving to the area? We'll have to set up a playdate for the dogs."

Alex looked at his dad. Dane smiled. "Sounds like a great idea. Someone in the family should be dating." He chuckled at his own joke.

Steve would do that, say something lame, then laugh because he thought it was funny. The action was such a man thing to do that she had to smile at him.

"So have you moved into town yet?"

"Yep, I rented one of the Val Verde townhomes. I start at the school next week. Since you're a nanny, do you have anyone you could recommend to pick Alex up from school? In Houston they had an after-school program, but here all they offer is a Wednesday program at the church. Which is great, but I need other days, too."

"Dad, I can hang out at the gym with you."

"Alex, we've talked about this. It's not safe."

She glanced at Garrett and found a stony expression that told her nothing. She faced the coach. "Let me think about it."

Dane glanced around the room. "Do you have paper so I can write down my number?"

"Pilar has fallen asleep. I need to go get ready for work, so I'll take her to bed." He held out a free hand to Dane. "I'm the local Texas state trooper. Nice to meet you, Coach. Hope you have a winning season."

"Thanks. And thanks for keeping our dog."

"Oh, that's all Anjelica." He held out his hand for his son. "It's bedtime. Say good-night for now. It sounds like you'll be seeing them again."

Anjelica held it together long enough to see Coco out to the car with her family. With a big smile and a wave, she sent them off into the night.

Chapter Ten

Standing on the edge of the porch, Anjelica watched as the taillights disappeared. A little boy had been reunited with his dog, and she would even see them again. Happy endings were good. There was no reason for the emptiness in her heart.

She would not cry. There was no reason to cry. Heading back into the house, she went straight to Esperanza's room. At the threshold she stopped. It wasn't her daughter's room anymore. It was a playroom for two children she took care of for someone else.

Garrett rocked Pilar, his voice carrying the words to "I Will Always Love You." Rio had fallen asleep on the area rug. Selena lay next to him.

Anjelica stood there and made herself breathe. It wasn't working. Her chest pulled tight, so she bit hard on the inside of her cheek.

Garrett looked up. "So Coco is off with her family." He kissed the sweet forehead of his little girl, the little girl she might lose.

No, not hers. Pilar was not hers to lose. She belonged to Garrett. Everything she loved belonged to someone else.

A sob broke her steady breathing and she forced

it back down. Rule number one, never cry in front of people; it made them feel uncomfortable.

She knew she was just a temporary caregiver of the dog and the little girl. They were never hers to begin with.

Garrett must have put Pilar down, because he was suddenly there. In the door frame with her. His large, strong hand on her arm.

"Are you all right?" He ducked his head down, trying to get her to make eye contact.

She couldn't. With a nod, she turned. Her room was too far away. She needed to get behind a closed door so she could fall apart in peace. That was how she got over Steve and Esperanza. She'd survive this, too. It was nothing compared to her other losses. *God, I'm so tired of just surviving.*

He caught her arm and gently turned her to face him. *No. No. No. Don't be nice to me. Don't talk to me.* "Don't" was all she managed. She didn't have the strength to pull away from the comfort he offered.

"Anjelica, it's okay." One tug and he had his arms wrapped around her. She was cocooned against his warmth.

That was it—the fight was over. Her right hand went under his arm and flattened against his shirt. Under the material, hard muscles covered his ribs, which protected the heart she could feel beating. Her other hand balled into a fist and pressed against his upper chest. The pain and fear that had been buried for the last few hours boiled up and poured over her well-tended walls. Poor Garrett. She sobbed.

One arm held her close, his hand soothing her hair. The other covered her angry fist and held it close to his chest. He whispered something, but she couldn't hear it over her own heart breaking.

Her greatest fear had happened. She broke down sobbing and couldn't stop. Her whole body went numb. Without Garrett holding her up, she'd have been a puddle on the rug.

Her feet went out from under her. Garrett, with one free arm, swept her up and carried her to the giant red overstuffed rocking chair.

Unaware of how long they sat there, Anjelica calmed down to hiccups. She sat up and wiped at his Marines T-shirt. It was so saturated with her tears that she had no chance of getting it dry.

"Sorry." The single word crawled up her raw throat. Her eyes ached. Her whole body felt beaten and bruised. "Sorry" was all she managed.

"Stop. You have nothing to be sorry for." His thumb wiped her cheeks. "Truthfully? You held me together as much as I held you." In the moonlit room, the sharp edges of his profile were highlighted as his head went back. He drove out a long heavy sigh.

"I didn't want to put Pilar in her bed. I didn't want to let her out of my arms. The thought that they might take her away…" He closed his eyes. "It's eating at me. Then Mr. America shows up to take your dog. Rio freaks. If you hadn't come in, I would've stayed in the rocker all night holding her."

He caressed her hair, his fingers moving in a soothing rhythm. She looked up at him and found his eyes still closed. If it weren't for the steady movement of his hands, she would have thought he had gone to sleep. Her grief had been so consuming she hadn't really thought about his worries. He was so fiercely protective that she should have realized he would want to fix her heart-aches.

She touched the firm pulse on the base of his neck with the tips of her finger. A soft sorrow of loss burned at the edges of her chest. Would this bring on his night-mares?

Her gaze took in the beautiful outline of his strong features. "I'm really sorry."

A growl rumbled from his throat. "Don't say you're sorry. Then I'd have to say it, and right now I'm too angry for a sincere apology."

Okay, so maybe it was time to change the topic. "Did you just call Coach Valdez Mr. America?"

His lips pulled into a lopsided smirk. "I guess I could have called him Mr. Football or All-American."

She sat up, away from his warmth, and pushed her palm against his chest. "Are you jealous?"

"He took your dog and tried to steal my nanny." He sounded like a three-year-old.

Was he serious? "You're messing with me, aren't you?"

"Maybe." A grin told her she'd been played.

"Well, I am more of the strong-silent-music-man kind of girl." She settled back down against his shoul-der. Here the world felt right.

"He worked hard to get your number. Was all slick about it, too. It's all about the dogs and kids, really? Did you fall for that?"

A strong hand with long fingers, a musician's hand, turned her face to him. The pulse in his neck picked up a faster beat. She watched, holding her breath as he lowered his head.

A tentative touch at first. His lips touched hers, ask-ing for permission. Leaning in, she gave it.

The kiss washed over her. Even though his lips stayed on her lips with a gentle pressure, her skin tightened. Sensations buried long ago came back to life.

From her bottom lip to the corner of her mouth, he explored every nuance of a kiss. She missed feeling cherished. But this was wrong. She pulled back. He let her go. Her traitorous heart grumbled that he didn't even try to stop her. On uncertain legs, she stood.

"It's been a rough day. It's also been a long time since I was kissed and I...I just..." She what? Didn't remember it being so all-consuming? That didn't seem fair to Steve's memory. Her skin tightened with goose bumps. Shivering, she wrapped her arms around her waist. Arms that had just been around Garrett.

He was not her type. She put more distance between them.

He stood and ran his fingers through his hair. "You're right. I need to get to work and put this day behind me. We need to focus on the children."

She nodded.

"I think it would be better for the kids to stay in their room tonight."

Another nod was all she could manage.

He gathered the children and Selena, and paused in the kitchen.

"Night, Anjelica."

She followed him to the door and watched as he went up the stairs. Was Garrett right in his opinion that the new coach had been trying to get a real date with her? If she was smart, she would call Dane Valdez, but now the thought of going out with another man seemed wrong.

Garrett was a lawman. One day he might not come home. There would be no saving her heart again.

Being alone was not a new feeling, but tonight, after being in Garrett's arms, it left her empty. Like those nights after she lost Steve and Esperanza. She'd been so empty with no one to hold.

Her phone vibrated. Looking at the screen, she saw it was Jewel. She had missed three calls already. She needed the distraction.

"Hi, Jewel. Sorry I missed your calls. What's up?"

"You just need to say thank you. I sent the most gorgeous guy your way. He's new in town, so you don't have to worry that we're related to him." Her closest sister laughed. "He also lost his wife, so you don't have to worry about the awkward dead-spouse talk."

Anjelica shook her head and grinned. One of the things she always loved about Jewel: she didn't tiptoe around the elephant in the room. Some people thought she was too blunt, but it was nice being with someone who just said what she was thinking.

"Yes, I met him. He came over tonight to pick up Bum… Coco."

"Oh no! He said he would drive over on Sunday! How did you look? Isn't he yummy and so sweet? He has already volunteered to work with the Christian Athletic Fellowship. And that boy of his is too cute. Did you hit it off? Did you trade numbers? I was hoping to give you a heads-up so you'd make sure to look good, not that you could ever look bad. I mean, on your worst days, you still outshine the rest of us. He said he needed someone to watch his son after school."

"Breathe, girl." As much as all the matchmaking upset her, she couldn't help but smile. Her sister had the best intentions, like everyone else in her life.

"Oh, sorry. So, did it go well?"

"He just came to pick up the dog. His son wouldn't let up until they stopped by. Rio got upset and hid, but we worked it out and plan on setting up a playdate so we can visit Coco."

"Wow, one meeting and you already have a date. I knew y'all would be perfect for each other."

"It's not a date."

"Um…let me see. Prearranged time and place to meet with a man. Sounds like a date to me. I'd take it."

"Then take it. Listen, I'm not sure about a man who waited so long to find his dog. I mean, it's been over a month. They just now started looking for her?" She put the phone on speaker and started braiding her hair. It was nice talking to someone she didn't have to over-analyze every feeling with.

Jewel continued. "They were down here looking for property to buy. You know, he's a new athletic direc-tor for next year. They thought Bumper, or Coco, was asleep in her crate."

One quick breath and she was still talking. "They thought they had lost her for good. But when they actu-ally got down here, he did some more digging. Being a single dad and relocating can't be easy. And you know that dog is crazy. So, I would say it's not his fault."

"Garrett didn't even know he had kids a month ago and he still remembered to get their dog."

"Oh, so that's how it is. Garrett's a better dad. I thought you were never going to date another man in uniform with a gun strapped to him, no matter how good-looking. And I quote."

"That's not how quotes work and I'm pretty sure I didn't even say that." Now she was starting to get a headache. "Anyway, I'm not interested in Garrett that way. His kids need full-time attention, and that's all I have time for right now."

"You might officially be a lost cause. You're surrounded by great-looking men that love their children and you don't have the time. I give up. You're the one that says trust God's will. Not sure you really believe that."

Anjelica flopped back on her pillow. "You might be right, but I won't rush anything."

"I'm not saying to start planning a wedding or even kissing—I'm saying you could go on a date. No kids or dogs or any other animal, just you and an adult male."

Anjelica groaned, thinking of the kiss she should *not* have been thinking about.

"Anjelica Ortega-Garza! You've been kissing someone. It has to be that gorgeous state trooper."

"It was an accident. We both agreed not to go there again."

"Accidental kiss? How does that happen? You fell and your lips landed on his? I know you. The only man you had ever locked lips with was Steve. So what happened, when and how was it?"

"All that matters is that it's never happening again. I'm not strong enough to live with the uncertainty of his job."

"He kissed you tonight? After you met the hot new coach? What a man thing to do."

Anjelica closed her eyes and sighed. "I tell you what I'm worried about and all you heard was your theory of why he kissed me? I've got to get some sleep. I'll see you Sunday."

"I'm sorry, sis. You know we all love you, right?"

"Yeah, I do. Love you. Night."

Anjelica put her phone on the nightstand and pulled

the comforter down. No one got it. They all thought she was strong. They didn't see her real self. She was one small heartbreak away from a total meltdown.

What she didn't know was whether it would come from Garrett or his kids.

Chapter Eleven

Garrett stood on the balcony. Moonlight dusted his sanctuary. Two nights ago, he had experienced the most nerve-racking kiss in his life, and now they were pretending it had never happened.

He needed to start looking for a new place to live. Peace was more important now than ever. Living so close to her was not calming in any way. How much longer would he be able to stay here, anyway? Rio and Pilar would need more room as they grew.

Leaning on the rail, he took another sip of coffee. The light of her studio shone past her porch. She enjoyed listening to his music while she worked. He stepped inside to pick up a sax. The act of creating arrangements used to calm him; when did it become about her?

Before he could produce one note, a cry came from the nursery.

Picking the fussy baby up, he pressed his lips to Pilar's forehead. An unnatural warmth came off her skin. She had a fever. Heat came off her little body.

He felt better equipped this time. Between the parenting classes and Anjelica, he knew he could take care of her tonight. Taking her temperature, he found it too high and gave her the liquid medicine like Anjelica had shown him.

In the rocking chair, she settled across his chest. That worked for a while, but she started crying again. She was dry and didn't want her bottle. It wasn't her teeth this time.

What if she was really sick? Should he take her to the emergency room, or would that be overreacting? Rio stayed by his side. His son somehow got wedged between Garrett's leg and the edge of the chair. He was sound asleep. Pilar whimpered on his shoulder.

There was no way he would be able to move if he needed to get up. She kept coughing, and her breathing didn't sound natural.

He leaned his head all the way back and looked at the ceiling.

Pilar coughed again. Now it sounded like there was something in her chest. She lifted her head and started whimpering again. Restless, she squirmed until she had wiggled out of his hold. It was hard to keep a gentle grip.

Pilar took hold of the bottle like she was starving when he offered it to her. They were supposed to stay on a feeding schedule, but if it would make her stop crying, he was all for it.

After a couple of pulls, she screamed and threw the bottle across the room. Rio woke up and went after it without hesitation. Rubbing his sleepy eyes with one hand, he offered her the bottle with the other. She slapped it, bowed her back and cried louder.

Garrett glanced at the door. Anjelica was just a staircase away. She would know what to do, but she wasn't working now and he needed to learn how to do this on his own.

He tried to ease out of the rocker so he could get his

phone, but Pilar threw herself back so hard he almost dropped her.

He held her with both arms, stroking her wild curls. "Shh…baby girl. We'll figure out what's wrong and take care of it."

Rio followed him to the living room and watched as he called the nurse hotline Pilar's doctor had given him. Maybe the boy was starting to trust him; he hadn't run to Anjelica yet.

After he went through all the symptoms with the nurse, she recommended that he take her to a small bathroom and fill it with steam. She was having a hard time breathing, and now he knew to feel for the rattling in her chest.

The nurse also made him an appointment for the morning.

Sitting on the edge of the tub, he almost fell asleep. Rio put a hand on Garrett's arm. The concern and old wisdom in the young eyes brought a wave of guilt.

Garrett forced a smile. "I'm fine, little man, just a little tired. The important thing is to get your sister comfortable so she can get some sleep. Tomorrow we'll take her to the doctor to see if she needs any medicine."

Rio nodded. A soft knock on the front door had them both turning.

"Garrett? Rio? Is everything okay?" Anjelica had come up the stairs to them. "I thought I heard Pilar crying."

The tension keeping his muscles coiled tight relaxed. Anjelica would know what to do. "We're all in the bathroom. Pilar couldn't breathe well, so I'm making steam." He adjusted Pilar to his other arm. She was relaxing and her breathing was already easier. "Come on in."

Anjelica eased into the small space. She smiled at Rio. "Selena is standing guard at the door." She sat on the other side of the small tub. "Why didn't you call me?"

"It's your night off, and after all the extra time you put in the last few days, I wanted to prove I could do this myself."

The steam in the room had Anjelica's hair hanging in loose curls. "I didn't do very well and ended up calling the nurse helpline. I'm not sure I'll ever get this parenting thing down."

With a soft laugh, she shook her head. "That's what good parents do—they call for help when they need it."

He nodded. If he kept looking at Anjelica, he would start thinking about that kiss again. It had been so long since he spent this much time with a woman. It had him off-kilter.

"I've got a doctor appointment for her in the morning. I need to call and get someone to take my shift."

"I can take her."

"No, I'm the one responsible for her. I'll—"

"Garrett, no one expects you to do this all by yourself. That's why I'm here. My family means it when they say to call them and ask for help. They know kids." She reached for him. Tender fingers stroked his wrist before she wrapped her hand around his. "They probably knew about this steam shower trick. You have a whole team and these babies deserve that. Don't deny them or yourself out of stubbornness or pride."

"There are single moms that do this all the time. My mom somehow managed to raise me and my sister without any help."

"That's not how it should be, though. Everyone should have a mighty Ortega army." She let go of him and moved to touch Pilar's forehead. "Look, I think it worked. She's fallen asleep and her skin feels normal."

He adjusted her on his shoulder, pressing his palm against her back. "No rattling. We did it, Rio. We helped her feel better." He sighed and stood.

Rio, leaning against Anjelica, smiled up at him.

"Come on, little man—let's put y'all back to bed."

As they headed to the nursery, Pilar gave a soft snore, followed by a hiccup from her crying. His heart twisted, and there was a horrible burning in his throat. It would be so easy to fail at parenting, and the stakes were too high. How could he be responsible for not only their well-being but their full development into adult life?

Laying her in the crib, he pressed his lips to her forehead. His hands looked so big as he tucked her in and said a little prayer. After making sure she would stay asleep, he picked up the rejected bottle and headed to the kitchen.

Anjelica poured milk into a pan. "I thought some warm milk would help us all get back to sleep. Rio, do you want chocolate in yours?"

With an energetic nod, his curls bounced around his face.

Garrett laughed. "Would the chocolate override the benefits of the warm milk? Rio, use your words."

"Yes, please."

Anjelica grunted with a smirk as she opened the pantry door. "Would you stir the milk?" she asked as she dug through the selves.

After checking the milk, Garrett turned his back to them and rinsed out Pilar's bottle. Working with Anjelica made everything better. There was no way he could have tackled fatherhood without her.

A loud crash and a child's cry had him spinning

around to face the source of such a sound. He lunged at the small boy standing too close to the threat.

Arms wrapped, holding the warm body to his chest, he rolled up against the wall. The boy's clothes were wet. Blood? Oh no! He was too late again.

"Garrett?"

Focus, Garrett. To keep everyone safe, you have to stay aware. The boy was crying. He was alive. Opening his eyes, he studied the boy. His son, Rio. Alive. Not… He blinked to clear his mind of the child he'd failed to protect in Afghanistan.

Garrett blinked. "Rio? Why does he have blood on him?"

"Garrett. It's just milk. There's no blood. Let me check him to make sure he didn't get burned."

Slowly getting to his feet, he checked Rio. "Did I hurt you?" He gently pulled the wet shirt off his son as he checked for any marks on the tender skin. "I don't think the milk had gotten hot yet." He ran his hand along the thin arms. "I'm so sorry, Rio. I didn't mean to scare you. I thought you were in danger."

Anjelica knelt beside them with a towel in her hand. "Come here, Rio. I'll dry you off. Your dad has a hero complex and is always ready to jump in and save us. Even from a pan of spilled milk." She looked the boy straight in the eyes. "Now, I do have a rule you need to follow so your dad doesn't go all ninja on us anymore. Stay away from the stove and don't ever reach up there and touch a pot, even if you're trying to help. When you are tall enough, I'll teach you how to handle the pots. Do you understand?"

Garrett closed his eyes. "I left the pot handle facing out." He reached for his son and pushed the damp curls back. "I'm sorry about that, Rio. I'll be more careful in the future."

Big gray eyes blinked. "You're not going to hit me?"

Anjelica stopped a soft gasp midway and covered her mouth.

"Rio, look at me. I will never hit you. If you do something wrong, we'll talk about it and figure out the consequence." How could a grown man treat a small child that way?

He stood and ran both hands through his hair. His heart and gut got so twisted he couldn't think. "Anjelica, do you mind washing him off and putting him to bed? The consequence tonight is no hot chocolate for any of us. I didn't put the handle in the right place, and Rio messed with something on the stove."

Anjelica looked at him with her bottom lip stuck out. "I wanted hot chocolate." She winked at him, and then her mouth eased into a smile.

Rio stood with his head down. "I'm sorry, Anjelica."

"We want you to be safe, Rio. No more touching anything on the stove or in the oven, okay?"

"Yes, ma'am."

"I'll wash him off and tuck him into bed." With a tenderness and understanding he did not deserve, Anjelica nodded at him while she herded Rio to the small bathroom.

He went to the sink and splashed cool water on his face. With a drink in hand, he slid into a chair at the small table. The juice vibrated as he raised it to his lips. He set the glass back down and pressed his forehead into his palms. His elbows dug hard into the tabletop, trying to stop the shaking.

He couldn't do this. Reality slipped too easily from

his mind. The kids were already too fragile. They needed someone they could rely on, and it wasn't him.

Anjelica helped Rio settle into his makeshift bed under Pilar's crib. Leaving, she paused in the door frame.

The whispered notes of Garrett's saxophone floated through the air. Eyes closed, she allowed the music to wrap around her.

God, give me the words to help heal all the hurts and confusion I know Garrett is trying to fight alone. Let him know You have him.

Moving all the way into the room, she listened. The pain and love moved from him through the sax and into the night. He stopped, setting the instrument back in its case, his profile highlighted by the moon.

"Sorry. When I don't know what else to do, I play."

"Don't apologize—it was beautiful. I do the same with my art. Getting my fingers in the clay helps me focus. Some of my best conversations with God happen in my studio."

He nodded. There had to be a way to reach him but still keep her distance. After that kiss, she needed to move carefully.

"Are you okay? You had another episode. Was it the noise of the pot that set it off?"

His jaw went stone hard as he stared out into the night. That was not the response she hoped for. "Garrett."

"I don't think I can do this. Maybe she would be better off with her grandmother. We don't know her. She might be perfect for Pilar."

Anger surged through her veins. "Now you're being an idiot."

That got his attention. Tonight his eyes looked more

gray than green as they narrowed at her. "That's your pep talk?"

"It's one in the morning. Being a parent is tough and you *will* make mistakes. You apologize, make it better and move on. You don't give up on them, or yourself."

She crossed her arms over her chest. The need to touch him, to soothe him, would only get her in trouble. *God, I need You to lead this.* "You know her place is with you and Rio. This is where she belongs. Are you going to give up Rio, too?"

Garrett turned from her and braced his hands on the railing. Clouds slid over the moon, engulfing the balcony in darkness.

Not able to stay away from him, she walked outside and placed her hand on his back. He tightened. "You are her father. Imagine packing her things and handing her over to them. People that didn't want her a month ago. People that don't want her brother. She's your daughter now. Do you think you could really just hand her over?"

He had a restlessness about him tonight. The ends of his hair stood up in different directions from his hands repetitively fussing with it. She loved how adorable it made him.

Not able to resist, she brushed it into place with her fingers, bringing her closer to him. The contact warmed her whole arm and traveled to her traitorous heart. Stepping back, she looked into the apartment. "Where's her sippy cup?"

"In the cabinet with the other cups. Why?" He followed her.

"If she has an ear infection, sucking on the bottle creates pressure. That was why she kept throwing it away. It hurt. We don't want her to get dehydrated, though. So when she wakes up, make sure she gets some water."

Turning, she had it in her hand, ready for him. "Are you over the delusion that giving her up is good for her?"

He grinned and nodded. The look made her want to cry. Why couldn't love be easy like it was in high school? "Your daughter is waiting for you, and I'm going back to my house. Good night, Garrett. I'll see you at seven."

One step at a time, she made it back to her room. The mountains of pillows and handmade quilts offered no comfort. She had lost her heart, and she doubted it would return unbroken.

Even if she gave in and accepted a lawman as her future, she didn't think his heart would be available.

As he filled the cup, he held it steady. That was an improvement. *Okay, God, You got me this far. What do I do now to keep them safe?*

Was he the best place for them? Shoulder leaning against the door, he paused. Rio's voice was low but clear. He was talking to his sister.

"I think it's going to be okay, Pilar. Our new daddy is nice and he doesn't yell or hit us, even when you cry a lot or when we mess up."

Every muscle tightened as he held himself still. The need to hit the man who caused all that pain was a waste of energy, but it still burned deep in his gut. Garrett heard a noise he couldn't identify.

"You like your room?" From the sound of his voice, Rio had moved.

Pilar answered with gurgling and the sweetest laughter that twisted his heart. How many of these late-night talks had happened when he thought they were sound asleep?

"Yeah, but it's for girls," Rio replied as if she had spoken in a clear language. "Maybe at your next birthday, if everything is still good, I'll stay in my bed. It's a race car, for a boy. Don't worry—I'll stay here as long as you need me. I promise not to leave you."

Garrett leaned the back of his head against the wall. Now he wanted to hug them close and cry over all the things he couldn't fix or wipe clean. Rio sounded like an old man, not a five-year-old. These were his children. His family. His responsibility to protect. His throat tightened. He could barely breathe.

Anjelica was right. He would never willingly turn either of these kids over to someone else. They were his. He was their father, and it was going to stay that way no matter what he had to do to make it happen.

He started forming a plan that would keep them all together. A plan to keep the kids safe. He hated that they might need to be protected from him. But they needed someone who could love them without hang-ups. Someone who would be steady when he fell apart. He imagined it would look better at court if he was married.

He softly knocked before going all the way in the room. He didn't want to scare Rio. "How's our princess doing?"

His son had gone mute again. Well, he'd talk to him when he was ready.

Now that he had the beginnings of a plan, the ache in his belly eased. He would trust that God had brought the kids to him for a reason. And as soon as he got Anjelica alone, he'd talk to her about the plan. This could work.

Chapter Twelve

Leaving the doctor's office, Garrett knew more about nebulizers than he did his own truck engine. Pilar breathed with ease now, and that was all that mattered. An antibiotic for the ear infection and a sucker for her brave brother made everyone better.

In Anjelica's house, they settled the kids in the playroom for their naps so he could head into work. This was the perfect time to talk to her about his plan. So why was he nervous? It was simple, and he couldn't imagine her not going along.

Then again, he didn't have a great track record in understanding women. Jake would be a good one to talk to first. See what he thought. He took another drink of coffee as Anjelica walked into the room. He needed to talk to her and stop putting it off.

"They're doing great. Fell asleep right away." For the trip to Kerrville today, she wore her hair in a ponytail.

"Before I head to work, there's something I want to talk to you about." He rubbed his jaw. "Want to sit in the living room?"

Her eyebrows wrinkled. "Sure. Is something wrong?"

He waited for her to sit on the chair with the chicken

pillow. Chickens—he never understood that. Glancing up, he realized she was staring at him, waiting.

"I'm worried I can't be here for the kids the way they need me." He paused, not sure what words to use to make her understand how important this was to him and the future of his family.

She tilted her head as if not understanding his words. "You've done a great job helping the kids feel safe." Standing, she left the chicken chair and sat next to him. "You were in a war zone—the things that happened, I can't even imagine. I've done some research and I think you need to find another vet, one you can talk to."

Keeping his face relaxed, he tried to hide the frustration at her suggestion. "Torres already suggested Reeves. I don't really see how that'll help." He stood and paced a few times before stopping at the window. "You've seen two episodes I've had where I lost track of reality. I can control it. I have for the last five years."

He moved to the bookshelf full of photos of her life. He wanted those kinds of roots for his little family. How much to tell her? Knots tightened in his gut when he even thought of what happened all those years ago. At times it seemed like yesterday. "I have a very important question to ask you. There's… I need you to know what happened so there aren't any misunderstandings."

She joined him, but when she reached out to touch his arm, he stepped away.

He never talked about what happened. There was no point. Not even to the required therapist. He told them just enough so they thought he felt a normal amount of guilt in order to get a clean bill of health.

"In Afghanistan one of our jobs was basically public relations. Establishing trust with people in the area.

One of the things we started doing was playing soccer with the local kids."

He paced behind the sofa, watching his boots cover the area rug as he went back and forth. A cold sweat coated his tight skin. She didn't need to know everything. Just enough so she would understand why the kids couldn't count on him 100 percent of the time.

"I actually enjoyed that part. It was like a little piece of home. Kicking the ball around with the kids. One boy I got closer to. He was about ten. I shared the candy my sister would send me. Somewhere along the way, he became mine. We both had a single mom and a sister to protect, being the only male in our families."

Interlocking his fingers behind his head, he sat down again and arched his back until he saw the ceiling. "Early one morning, I was running late to the field. A couple of the other guys were already there. The wind was sweeping sand across the flat landscape. I saw…"

He hadn't spoken the boy's name since giving the initial reports. Everything inside twisted at the memory of the tracks of his tears on dust-covered cheeks.

"As soon as I saw him, I knew something was wrong."

He licked his lips. He had worked so hard to shut down these images, locking them in a box and burying the incident so deep it wouldn't impede his life in Texas.

"Garrett?" So soft, her voice lashed at the fog that started to creep through his brain, the fingers of hopelessness reaching to control him. She moved to sit next to him, her hands clasped in her lap. "It's all right."

"No, it's not. They had gotten to him. Probably threatened his family." He should have known. Should have warned the kid. Done something to protect him.

He clenched his fists. The tension caused his arms

to shake. "I knew. In my gut I knew what was about to happen, and I just stood there."

Warm skin intertwined with his. He took a deep breath and focused on her touch. She anchored him back down into the living room in Clear Water, Texas.

"He stood on the far side of the field. Kids ran around him, laughing as their loose shirts flapped in the wind. A few of the other guys that played with the kids were there."

He tried to swallow, but his throat tightened. Dry, no moisture. The kid needed him, and he had just stood there. Frozen.

Her hand squeezed his wrist. He took a chance to look at her. He found her gaze searching his face. "It wasn't your fault."

"I just stood there and did nothing when the device went off."

"For how long?"

"What?"

"From the time you got there to the time it... How long were you there? What could you have done?" Tears hovered on her bottom lashes. Her lips drew taut. "It's unimaginable. But how could you have changed what happened? How does it make you less of a father? That's what this is about, right? You explaining why you can't be the perfect father."

There was no way she would ever understand, and that was okay. She was protected from that kind of evil. "I should've known he'd be marked by the men hiding behind legitimate business. He was mine and they used him."

"I still don't understand how you could have changed that day."

"When the... I should have—" he pushed the hair

back from his forehead and closed his eyes "—protected him. He was mine. Killed on my watch. Along with two other kids and a marine. A buddy of mine lost his arm. I didn't even have a scratch. I just stood there on the other side of the field."

"So what could you have done? Run across the field and disabled the bomb?"

He sighed and stood. He needed space. This was why he never bothered to talk about it. "You don't get it. I failed to protect them. I could've at least run to him and wrapped him up against me. Used my body to absorb the explosion. The other marine would've made it home. Boys would've seen their next birthdays. He wouldn't have died standing alone and scared."

"And you would have died. It's tragic what happened, and horrible. But if you weren't here, what would have happened to Rio and Pilar? They are safe and together because you are here, protecting them."

"That's not the point." He heard her move. She followed him to the window.

"You're right—it's not fair. The things that happen, why they happen, don't make sense. You can't focus on one part without looking at the big picture."

His jaw started to hurt.

"What you saw was horrific. Your strength amazes me."

Her hand rested on his shoulder blade. He stiffened, fighting the urge to turn and wrap himself in her warmth. He had been so cold for so long.

"I'm not strong." He stepped away from her and leaned against the frame of the window seat, trying to look casual. "You're the hero. The one with the real strength. You've kept your faith and your smile through the loss of your husband and baby."

Not able to resist any longer, he reached out and touched her wet cheek with the back of his knuckles. "You, Anjelica Ortega-Garza, are the hero. That's why…"

Long, restless steps took him away from her and back to the sofa. Once again sitting, he gestured for her to join him on the couch. She moved to the red chicken chair instead.

"Okay. There's a reason I wanted to tell you this. It wasn't about getting your sympathy, but for you to understand my limits and why the proposal I'm about to give you is so important to Rio and Pilar. I need you to know why I can't do this alone."

She sat forward, her elbows resting on her knees. "You're not alone."

"But I need a permanent safeguard for the kids." He feared she didn't understand what he was trying to tell her. "Sometimes I see Rio and all I see is…the boy I lost. I want to set up a safety net."

"You have me and all the Ortegas."

"Right, but you're just the nanny, the hired help. I know you're more than that, but in a court of law, that's all they'll see. A single bachelor. If… When I get custody, you'll have no legal rights." He rubbed his palms against his eye sockets. *Just say it. It's a good plan.*

Leaning forward, he looked her straight in the eyes. "I want us to get married. It will give us an edge over a single grandmother Then you can adopt them and they'll have you as their legal parent. You'll be their mother."

Her mouth open and her eyes wide, she recoiled as if a scorpion had fallen from the ceiling.

Give her time to process. He licked his lips again.

Like a spring, she popped up. She moved around and

put the chair between them, looking at him as if…as if he had gone crazy.

"Did you just ask me to marry you so I can be the mother of your children?"

He wasn't feeling good about the tone of her voice. "Yes, it's the surest way I can think of to provide them with everything they need. Unconditional love and security. We'd all live here in this house. Children need those things, especially Rio and Pilar. They need you."

"You want us to get married so that I can be a legal guardian of your children and provide the love that you can't give them? Because you want them to live in my home?"

"It's not that I don't love them. I just can't love them the way you can. You do love them, don't you?" Standing, he went around the overstuffed chair and stopped in front of her. He had to get her to understand. "This is a perfect solution for the kids. It's not all an act for your job, is it?"

"Garrett… I do love them." She touched his face. Tears hung on her eyelashes. "You're such an incredible man. You never hesitated to bring two children into your life once you knew they needed you."

Her gaze roamed over his face as if looking for something she'd lost. "That might be the biggest problem. I could easily love you. My heart would be wrapped up in you so fast…but you don't want my heart, do you? You just want me to love your children." She stepped back and shook her head. "I can't be in that kind of marriage. It would destroy me."

Heat burned his gut. He had to fix this. He had to make her stay. "I can't be a father without you."

"You want to love everyone at arm's length because it's safer for you."

Now there was a hint of anger in her voice. Somehow he'd messed this all up and needed to fix it. "It's not about me."

"Yes, this is all about you. How *you* might fail them. How *you* can't love them enough. How *you* can't be the perfect father. Guess what—humans make mistakes. None of us are perfect, not a single one of us. It can't be an excuse to stop trying. To stop giving. Your kids deserve all of you."

She crossed her arms around her waist. A sob broke up her breathing. "Whoever your wife will be deserves all of you. Not a watered-down shadow of the man you're afraid of being."

The tears fell freely now. "You have to figure out how to let people in and trust them with your broken parts, or you'll never be whole enough to love someone."

"You want me to say I love you? Should I have brought flowers and gotten on one knee? That's what I did for Viviana. Would that make all the ugliness better?"

Restless, he started pacing behind the sofa. Each step full of the anger at all the people he had loved. "My mother loved my father. She did everything to keep him. She also spent hours crying. I loved Viviana with every fiber of my being and told her that every time we were together. I gave her everything I had, and look where that got us. A mess with a little boy who didn't trust the world enough to speak."

He stopped and glared at Anjelica. She wanted something that didn't exist. "What I'm offering you is respect and friendship. I could say the words if it'll make you feel better. But we both know they don't mean anything."

Her eyes were now red and puffy as she wiped at the

tears. He stood, feet planted. He would not give in to her. That was what he always did with his mother and Viviana. "I won't let you manipulate me with tears."

A rough laugh sounded from her soft lips. "Oh, Garrett. I hate that I'm crying right now." She wiped her hand on her jeans. "Believe me, if I could, I would dry them up and walk out. I would, but I can't. I also can't make you feel something you don't. I do love your children."

Her hand motioned toward the nursery. "They own my heart as if I'd given birth to them myself, but I will not marry you just to be their mother. You have been through some inhumane events. Please talk to someone about it. Someone who will understand everything you've been through."

"I don't need to talk to anyone." He crossed his arms over his chest.

"There's nothing wrong with asking for help! I spent many hours talking and listening in a grief group."

That sounded worse than his nightmares. He looked at the pictures on the shelf behind her. "There are parts of me so broken I can't give you the kind of marriage you want. I think there might be a war in me I can't win."

"I believe that God has the ability to fix the most broken clay pot. If only we decide to give it to Him." Turning her back to him, she walked over to her books. "I understand broken. I've been there in my own way." Her fingertips brushed along the spines until she came to a black leather book.

With the book in hand, she stood a foot from him. He could smell sweet vanilla and gardens.

"Here, take this. I've marked passages that helped me. Without God, I don't think I could have gotten out of bed. Let alone love again. I do see a marriage in my future, but it will be with two whole hearts that aren't afraid of scars and broken pieces."

His jaw ached with tension. "So why do you keep your scars covered? Are you ashamed of them?" As soon as he asked the question, he wanted to take it back.

The hurt in her eyes cut him. Her delicate hand went to the base of her throat, flattening the multicolored scarf she wore today. Her dark skin went a tint lighter.

Arm extended to her, he needed to take the pain away. The pain he had caused. She stepped out of his reach. "I'm sorry. That was a jerk thing to say." His arms ached to hold her. The years living with Viviana had taught him how words could hurt. He didn't want to be that person. "I'm sorry."

"No, you're right. I still have broken parts and fears I don't want to face. Life is not easy." She pulled the scarf off and wrapped it around her hand. "The scar is from the car accident that caused the death of my baby girl."

He couldn't stand it, being so far away from her after he was the one who caused her suffering. As gently as he could, he pulled her to the couch. She wouldn't look at him, but she followed.

"You don't owe me anything. It was none of my business to begin with, and I'm truly sorry for what I said. If there was a way to take it back, I would."

"I know." She shrugged. "As many times as I've asked for forgiveness, you'd think I'd be over it by now, but you're right. There's a part of me that hangs on to the guilt. They delivered the news about Steve. I shouldn't have been driving, but nothing would stop me. I'll probably never get completely over it."

Slowly, Anjelica rose and walked over to the picture of her late husband. "I promised Steve I would take care of our baby girl and made him promise not to play the hero. He pledged to come back home to us. We both failed."

She stood silent for a while before turning back to him. Maybe this was it—she would see how life was too short and she would change her mind about his proposal.

"Everyone kept telling me he died a hero. How I should be so proud of him." Her mouth was firm, all tenderness gone. Golden eyes now clear of tears, she stood straight, her chin up. "To tell the truth, I was angry. Another reason a marriage between us would never work. I can't live with another hero. A man that rushes into danger with a gun strapped to his body."

She shook. "Your guilt is you didn't react fast enough. That you didn't die that day and others did." A lopsided pull of her lips that formed a warped illusion of a smile became the saddest expression. "I can't sit at home wondering whose life you might save at the risk of your own. That sounds really selfish of me, but I can't do that again. We each have broken parts." She played with the edge of her scarf. "I realize it's so much easier to say 'hand it over to God' than to actually hand everything over. Yes, there are bits and pieces of me that clutter the floor, but I know my limits." A sigh heavy with sadness left her lips. "Marriage to a lawman that won't even love me? That's a line I cannot cross, not even for those precious babies."

There was a new weight on her shoulders he feared he had placed there.

She shrugged. "Maybe Steve didn't love me enough to play it safe, but he did love me completely while I had him. I deserve that kind of love, and so do your kids."

Picking up her sweater on the back of the chair, she

looked at the pictures on her shelf. "I'm tired. I think I'll take a nap while Rio and Pilar are asleep. I'll have them up in your apartment with dinner ready when you get home. As soon as you get in, I'm leaving. I think I'm going to stay with my mom for a little bit. I need some clear boundaries."

Acid burned his stomach. "Don't worry about dinner. I can make it. Do what you need to. Will you be here for breakfast in the morning?"

She shook her head. "I'll be here right before you leave for your shift in the afternoon. I think our morning cups of coffee need to stop."

He wanted to yell and throw something. Instead of guaranteeing she would always be here for the kids, he'd pushed her away. He had to make her stay, but he didn't know how.

Maybe he did need to talk to someone. He looked at the Bible she had given him. Pink flags of paper stuck out. She was so different from his mother and Viviana that he didn't know what to say or do to make it right.

"All right." He wanted to tell her no, that he needed her as much as the kids did, but she made it clear. A personal relationship would not work between them. Why couldn't she just let things stay the same? Teeth clenched, he fought the longing to reach out to her. Why did she want love to complicate their relationship?

She glanced at the clock. "It's time for you to leave if you're going to get to work on time."

With a nod, he turned and headed out the door. Making sure the screen door didn't slam, he eased it closed. He stood on the other side and watched her disappear into her bedroom.

The Bible she gave him was still in his hand. She claimed he would find answers in this leather-bound book. The plan had been to move into the future together, but now it was even more insecure.

He'd thought his proposal would be a win for both of them. Well, for him, anyway. All she would be getting in the trade was a messed-up husband who couldn't love her and two kids who weren't hers. She was smart to run, but it didn't mean he had to like it.

Anjelica buried her head in her pillow to muffle any sound and sobbed. Her whole body shook.

Without meaning to, Garrett had ripped her heart out.

She was in danger of losing her resolve to stay away from heroes. Telling him she could easily fall in love with him was a lie.

Without a doubt, she already loved him. In so many ways this feeling was deeper than the easy friendly first love she'd had for Steve. They had grown up together. They were friends years before they dated.

Garrett made her feel things in a new way, and that made him even more dangerous. He was so intense.

Raising her head, she pulled the tissues from her nightstand and attempted to clean her cheeks.

Her phone vibrated. Ignoring it, she covered her face with a pillow. If it was Garrett, she might give in and ask him to come back. It had been so tempting to say yes. To be his wife and a mother to two little ones who needed her.

In her core, the truth burned. If she stepped in and took care of everyone, he would never trust himself to be the father she knew he already was. Those babies would never fully know how much he loved them, because he was too afraid to believe it. He didn't know how strong he really was in his weakness.

But if she did say yes, they would be hers for real and she would be there for them every "good morning" and every story time.

She sat on the edge of her bed and looked out the window, where a giant oak tree had stood for a hundred years. Its wide base twisted and turned as it reached up and out, growing stronger through the storms.

Not able to resist, she gave her phone a sideways glance. "Unknown." Curious, she picked it up and read the text.

Hi. It's Dane Valdez. New coach. Alex's dad. He's been asking when he can meet up with Rio and play. He says Coco is missing y'all.

The new coach and his son had been at church. He seemed like a nice guy with a nice job. Was Garrett right that Coach Valdez would ask her out if given the opportunity? He fit the bill for what she thought she wanted, but her heart was not in it. She feared it had already found a home.

There had to be a way she could be there for Rio and Pilar without losing herself in the bigger-than-life hero Garrett Kincaid.

All right, the pity party had to be over. With her grandmother's Bible in hand, she turned to familiar pages and prayed.

Chapter Thirteen

Opening the refrigerator, Garrett tried to decide if he needed milk for cereal or if he'd go for a full plate of eggs and bacon. Anjelica believed the day didn't start if you didn't have bacon.

This would be their first morning without her.

Cereal had less risk involved. Man, he couldn't even commit to a breakfast. "Rio, do we go with cereal or eggs and bacon?"

He glanced over to the door and found his son staring out the window toward the big house.

"Sorry, little man, but Anjelica won't be joining us this morning."

Rio turned and glared at him. Going back to standing watch, he pressed his hands against the window. "She's gone like Mommy?"

His heart dropped as he stopped what he was doing to go to Rio and take him in his arms, pressing his lips against the messy hair. "No, no. She's fine. Don't worry. She'll be back later this afternoon. Whenever I go to work, she'll be here for you." Rio turned his back to him, as if ignoring his words would make his nanny appear.

"Hey, so what is it, cold or hot?"

Rio shook his head.

Garrett went ahead and scrambled some eggs. He almost burned the bacon, but everyone ate without complaint.

Pilar actually smiled and giggled. Rio ate in silence, glancing to the door.

Anger simmered as Garrett replayed their discussion. Anjelica said he didn't love them, or her, enough. He couldn't imagine loving them more. That was why he wanted to provide them with security only she could bring to them.

Washing the plates in the sink, he scrubbed a little harder than necessary. Done with that chore, he turned and looked at the kids. His skin felt too tight.

Normally when he got like this, he'd go for a run, but he didn't have a stroller that carried both kids. He needed something more physical than his music.

Both of the kids were playing in the middle of the living room. Rio stacked blocks and Pilar knocked them over. Their laughter over the simple action tugged at him.

He needed something to knock over. Glancing out the window, the pile of wood from the fallen trees gave him an idea.

"Come on, guys. We're going outside to split some wood." He gathered up Pilar and bundled the toys in the blanket. "We need some fresh air."

With everyone settled a safe distance away, next to the garden, Garrett attacked the wood with the ax. Between each hit, he glanced at his children. One of Anjelica's bunnies was checking out Rio. Garrett paused to make sure the boy was gentle. A goat came to the edge of the fence and tried to get their attention. The heaviness on his chest lightened.

Each swing carried less anger. *God, You brought me to this point.* Whack. *You put Anjelica in my path.* Whack. *How do I fix it?* Whack.

If he could get Anjelica on his team, everything else would fall into place. If he had a complete family to offer them, the courts wouldn't take Pilar.

His arms and shoulders burned. Never before had he seen such a clear vision of what he wanted his future to look like. Years ago he had wanted a perfect family.

He'd done everything in his power to make Viviana fit into that image. It hadn't been real. Then in Afghanistan, he failed to protect…Sayid. There, he'd said the boy's name.

He was not strong enough. Whack.

This time, he saw Rio jump, moving closer to his sister as she let the goat nibble on her fingers.

He was an idiot. Got a kid who watched his mother be beaten, sure take him outside and swing an ax around. What was he thinking? Another reason he couldn't be trusted. What if he had?

Garrett leaned the ax against the tree stump and walked over to the kids. Going down to the ground, he rested his arm over his knee. "You okay, little man?"

His son kept his gaze down as he pulled the floppy-eared bunny into his lap. Selena raised her head and looked at Garrett. Reaching across Rio, he scratched her under her chin.

"Are you still worried about Anjelica coming back?" Garrett waited. Rio had gone mute again. He sighed in frustration and raised his hand to push his hair back but stopped midway when the boy flinched.

Slowly, he put his arm down. "Rio, I'm not going to hit you. I told you that and I always keep my promises. Have I lied to you yet?"

He kept his head down, and the curly hair bounced with each shake. "But you're angry." Rio's words were so low Garrett had to strain to make each one out.

A short snort escaped. "You're one smart kid. I thought I hid it well. But yes, I'm angry. There was something I wanted and I didn't get it. That's why I came outside to chop wood."

Needing to touch Rio, he brushed the wild curls back. Haircut next day off. "We all get angry. It's a normal emotion. It's not the anger that's bad—it's what we do with that anger that can hurt others or ourselves. If we hold it inside, it'll burn a hole in our gut, or we'll explode and hurt those around us."

Rio petted the rabbit, which appeared to have gone to sleep. His eyes, too old for a five-year-old, made Garrett want to weep. "James yelled and threw things when he got angry."

His arms longed to pull his son into his lap. He had so many hurts and injustices to fix. "Rio, listen to me." He waited for the boy to look at him. "I promise to never hit you, and if I start yelling, you can ask me to stop. No matter what you do, no matter how big your mistake or accident is, I will love you. I might get mad and there will be consequences, but everything I do is for you. So you can grow into the best man possible."

"Will I be like you?"

"You'll be Rio Kincaid." He smiled and ruffled the mop of hair. "A better version of me."

"Pilar's dad said I was a waste of no-good space and I should crawl into a hole and die. He didn't like my voice."

Oh, Viviana, why? No longer able to keep space between them, he pulled Rio against him. "The best day of my life was the day I found out about you. Then I saw you. You were so brave, protecting your sister. I love you, Rio, and I'm so proud you're my son. You're a gift from God, and just because James was too…angry about life to see it, does not make it less true. Do you understand?"

Against his heart, he felt the slight nod. He didn't have the words to explain to his son how important he was to him. "You're mine, Rio, and I'm yours. God gave us to each other, and we have to be grateful every day for that." He swallowed emotions so strong they hurt. "It's okay to get angry. You just have to find good ways to get it out."

"Like chopping wood?"

He laughed. "Yeah, but you have to be taller than the ax before you swing it. I do have an idea, though." At that moment Pilar slowly fell to her side. "Oh, look, we bored her to sleep."

Rio giggled. "She's too little to get angry. She just sleeps, plays and eats."

Scooping up his daughter and cradling her in one arm, he took a moment to look at her tiny soft features. There was no way he was giving her up. She was as much his as Rio was. "Let's put her in the playpen, and I'll get the things we need to let go of our anger."

It took them a while, and putting water in balloons was harder than it looked. But he had Rio laughing, so the task was worth the humiliation and soaked clothes.

He tossed a water-filled balloon in the air. "Now, the thing is, you throw the balloon as hard as you can against the garden fence. You can roar like a lion if you want. With each throw, you get rid of an angry thought. Ready?"

He handed his son a balloon. "Don't hold back. Give it everything you got."

Rio tossed the red balloon just like Garrett had done. He narrowed his eyes and set his jaw, pulling his arm, and let a loud bellow out that bounced off the hills as he threw the balloon.

The pile of balloons got shorter and the garden fence was dripping with water. Rio's laughter was the best. The therapist had him drawing out his feelings, but sometimes a boy just needed to be physical.

They both turned at the sound of a vehicle pulling into the drive.

Rio took off running. "Anjelica!"

Garrett stayed close. It was too early to be Anjelica, but maybe she had changed her mind. As they rounded the corner, Rio stopped midstride. In order not to run over him, Garrett braced the little shoulder and jumped to the side.

An unfamiliar gray Civic pulled up to the house.

Rio slid behind him and grabbed his leg. "Is she here to take me?

A tall willowy woman stepped out and pushed her long red hair over her shoulder. Her name cut into his throat. Gloria, his mother, had shown up. Even at the age of fifty, she had the lost-princess look down pat.

She gave him a nervous wave, her pink lips forming a stiff smile.

"It's okay, Rio. The lady is my mother." He took Rio's hand and met Gloria Kincaid halfway across the yard.

Her hands interlocked in front of her. "Garrett. Surprise." She opened her palms before crossing them over her middle again. Her green-gray eyes, the same he saw in the mirror and in the sadness of his son's gaze, glanced down at Rio. His son was hiding behind him again.

With tears threating to spill over her lashes, she glanced between them. Rio stared at her with open wonder.

The minute he saw the picture of Rio, he'd recognized the eye color all three of them shared. It had been a bit eerie. What startled him now was what else his son and mother shared. In their eyes there was the same "I've seen too much, felt too much, loved too much" depth.

"She's your mom?" his son whispered.

Garrett picked him up and held him on his hip. "Hi, Mom. Yes, this is your grandmother."

Gloria covered her mouth and gave a sound that might have been a laugh or a gasp. Wiping her eyes, she gave Rio a smile. "You look so much like your dad when he was a little boy. You're so beautiful. Can I hug you?" She took a step forward.

Rio burrowed deeper against his chest, turning his face away from her.

"That's okay. You don't have to hug me. I can't believe I have a grandson. How about you call me GiGi. That sounds fun, doesn't it?"

"Mom, you have a granddaughter, too. I'm going to court to adopt his sister." He put his hand over Rio's ear and waited for her to say something. When she nodded and smiled, relief loosened his shoulders. "Why don't we go around back? She's asleep in her playpen. Don't want her to wake up alone."

"Pilar, right?" Her light laughter followed him. "When you jump into being a father, you don't hold anything back."

"They're great kids."

"Oh, I brought something for you. Let me get it from the car and I'll join you."

After checking on Pilar, they settled into the double rocker and waited.

"Your mom's pretty."

Before Garrett replied, Gloria walked around the corner with a purple flower-printed box. He frowned. He remembered that box always being in a closet wherever they lived at the time.

"Why, thank you, Rio. That's the cutest name." She set the box on the wicker table and went straight to Pilar. Rio slid down and stood next to the playpen with Selena.

"Your sister is just about the most precious thing I've ever seen. I can't wait to hold her when she wakes up." She turned back to Garrett. "I can see why you lost your heart to her. She looks just like her mamma."

A deep breath in relaxed his muscles. It was a good thing he spent his anger earlier today.

"Mom. Why are you here? On the phone the other day you suggested I let the state take care of the kids."

She bit her bottom lip and rubbed her hand on the front of her long skirt. "I was wrong. I just know the pain… That's not why I'm here. I brought the box that has all your school stuff. There are pictures of you and Viviana. I thought Rio would like to see you and his mother together. Children need to know there were happy times."

He raised one disbelieving eyebrow at her but didn't say anything.

She glanced at Rio before leaning toward Garrett. "You know I worried Viviana would hurt you again. She loved trouble, and you loved getting her out of it." She reached for his hand, and her long fingers intertwined with his. "I don't know how it all ended, but I do know it was not a lack of trying on your part."

He glanced at her hand. "Mom? What's with the ring?"

Her face lit up. "Oh, um, Hank asked me to marry him. I'll tell you all about him later. Today is about you, Rio and Pilar. Garrett, I'm so sorry for not being a better mother."

"Mom—"

She lifted another picture out. "There are a few of your father, too." Twisting around, she talked to Rio. "Your grandfather was such a good-looking man. Just like you and your daddy."

"I thought you had destroyed everything that had to do with Dad."

She passed the photo to Garrett, then started digging into the box again. "Not everything. Sometimes I worry that my anger might have destroyed parts of you."

Okay, now he was officially freaking out. "Mom, what's going on? Are you sick?" This was the kind of thing that people did when they found out they were dying. "You don't have cancer, do you?"

Her hearty laughter surprised him. Rio left his sister and crawled up in Garrett's lap.

Gloria patted Rio on the leg, and her laughter trailed off, leaving a soft smile. The one Garrett lived for as a kid. "No. What I have is a grandson I want to know. And a granddaughter. I also have a fiancé saying I need to unpack my past and move forward with a clean vision of what I want for the future." She pulled the box into her lap. "I want my family to be happy and know that, despite my mess-ups as a mom, they can count on me."

"You didn't mess up. Since my own very short journey of being a single father began, I've thought of you several times. You did an amazing job with us. As kids, we didn't appreciate the sacrifices."

He opened his palm and wrapped his fingers around hers when she accepted his invitation to join them. He pulled her in next to him on the double rocker. With Rio wedged in on one side, his mother reached across and brushed the curls out of the boy's face.

"He looks so much like you it hurts. Now I'm crying for real." Using the tips of her fingers, she wiped under her eyes. "Is my mascara running?"

"Does my hair make you sad, GiGi?" Rio had the side of his face pressed against Garrett's chest, but he hadn't moved away from her touch this time.

"No, sweetheart. It just makes me think of your dad when he was little. I'm so proud of him, and you make me think of all the time that has gone by and how grown-up he is now. A father to his own son and daughter. Sometimes mammas make a mess out of raising up their babies, but it doesn't mean they don't love them."

"Mom, you did a great job. We always had a safe place and something to eat. You taught us to stand on our own, to be independent. Why all this...?"

Tears welled up in her eyes, hanging heavy on her lashes. "How did you end up becoming such a good man?"

The sound of a vehicle pulling into the front drive interrupted any words he was going to say. Rio had drifted off to sleep on his shoulder, but now he had his head up and was looking at Garrett.

He nodded. "My guess is it's Anjelica's truck, but I'm not sure. Come on—let's check it out."

"I'll stay here and watch Pilar." His mom lifted the lid of the box. "Is Anjelica the one helping with the kids?"

He nodded. "She's also my landlord."

This time, instead of stopping at the corner of the

house, Rio picked up speed and launched himself at Anjelica. "I missed you so much!"

Her eyes went wide and she stared at Garrett. "Rio, honey, I love you. But don't worry if I'm not around for every breakfast." She wrapped her arms around him. He clung to her like a koala on a tree. With her arms holding him against her heart, she looked at Garrett. "Is everything all right?" Her gaze darted to the new car.

Garrett wanted to point out that she could be, maybe even should be, Rio's mother, but now was not the time for that discussion.

"Yolanda called and said Maria saw a strange car pull into the drive and stay." Worry clouded her eyes. "Does it have to do with the case?"

"It's my GiGi," Rio whispered as if unsure if it was good news or not.

"My mother arrived unannounced. She's on the back porch."

Anjelica swallowed and forced a smile. His mother had arrived. He wouldn't be needing her anymore. *Okay, Anjelica, this is not about you.*

"That's great, Garrett."

"God's timing, right? See, I've been reading the Bible you gave me. Since you want more space, my mother can watch the kids."

She pressed her lips to Rio's forehead. Eyes closed, she roped in her emotions. "So is she staying?" Being replaced so easily hurt, but what else could she do?

"Yes, but I don't know for how long. She said she's here to help and—" he winked at Rio "—she wants to get to know her grandchildren."

Rio nodded. "I'm her first grandson, and Pilar is her first granddaughter. She said Daddy jumped in fast."

It was the first time she'd heard Rio call Garrett Daddy. Her gaze rushed to Garrett. She saw a sense of wonder fall across his face. He blinked hard a couple of times.

"Yep. That I did. Best day of my life, bringing you and your sister home."

With a big smile and a vigorous nod that caused his curls to bounce, he hugged Anjelica's neck. "Daddy and I were throwing away our anger."

She sent Garrett a questioning look. What had they been up to? "Rio's a fountain of words." She pulled him close in a tight hug. "I love the sound of your voice."

"Daddy said you did. He said he did, too, and that I shouldn't hide it."

Oh, great. She was going to meet Garrett's mom crying. "Well, he's right. Want to introduce me to your GiGi?"

He wiggled down and took her hand. With his other one, he reached for Garrett, weaving his small fingers with his father's strong ones.

With them joined as one, the little boy pulled them forward. She didn't dare look at Garrett, worried he'd see the weakness in her eyes. Her throat burned.

On the back porch, Selena sat tall on the top step, standing guard. Her tail thumped against the boards when she saw them.

A storybook princess stood and smiled at her. Garrett's mother looked as if she had stepped out of a fairy tale. Anjelica wasn't sure why, but she'd pictured her as more of a worn-out biker chick.

"Hello." She approached them with her hand out. "I'm Garrett's mother. Gloria."

"Mom, this is Anjelica Ortega-Garza. She's been helping with Rio and Pilar. I really couldn't have done it without her. This is her house. We live in the apartment above the garage."

"Oh, this house is perfect. I always dreamed of having wraparound porches."

"I tried trading houses with him, but he can be a bit stubborn when it comes to letting people help."

Rio looked in the box. Holding a picture in both hands, he brought it close to his face. "It's Mommy. She looks like a princess." An edge of confusion lined his low voice. "Is that you with my mommy?"

Gloria moved to sit on the padded bench. "They're at prom. Your parents were friends since they were ten years old. Her family lived next door in one of the apartments we moved to." She dug in the box and found another picture. "Here they are at their first middle-school dance. Your mother was a very pretty girl. You can see where your sister gets that dark curly hair."

"Daddy's so little. He's shorter than Mommy."

Garrett sat on the other side and took the picture. "I told you I was a scrawny kid. I didn't start growing until I was sixteen."

"And then he didn't stop. He was so hungry all the time. I'd feed him a full meal and twenty minutes later he wanted to know what was for dinner." She laughed and smirked at Garrett. "Paybacks are coming your way."

Anjelica stayed at the bottom of the steps. She wanted to be part of that family, but they weren't hers. She had told him no. "Hey, guys. Let me take a picture of you, and then I'll be going back to town."

"Oh, I would love that." Gloria scooted closer to Rio and reached behind him to put her hand on Garrett's shoulder.

Rio tucked his chin and gave her a tentative smile.

After a few pictures, Garrett stood. "Can I talk to you before you leave?"

"Sure." Nerves knotted her stomach. She gave Garrett's mother a hug as she handed back her phone. "It was a pleasure meeting you, and I have a room upstairs for you to use."

"Is that all right with your husband?"

"There's no husband."

"Oh? You live in this big house all by yourself?"

"Mother. Don't. She doesn't date men with guns." Garrett placed his hand on the small of Anjelica's back and gently ushered her away. "Thanks for offering my mom a room."

Being alone with him was not good for her. She didn't want to hear any bad news. "What happened with Rio? He's talking, I mean really talking."

"He was worried when you didn't join us for breakfast."

"Oh, Garrett." She stopped as they passed the corner of the house. Next to the tree that shaded the old nursery. "I'm so sorry. I never meant to upset him."

"I know. We worked it out. What really bothered him was my anger. I thought I hid it, but apparently not. I was chopping wood and he wasn't sure what to do. We ended up talking about anger and how to handle it so we don't hurt the people we love or ourselves." After explaining his unexpected therapy, he grinned at her. "I never dreamed my five-year-old son would be teaching me about life." Garrett put his hands in the front pockets of his jeans.

"Throwing water balloons and roaring like lions sounds like it worked."

He nodded and looked toward the front gate. "We

have the court date in three days. Are you still going with us?"

"I would love to. If it's all right with you."

His gaze stayed on the horizon. She wished she knew what he was thinking. Guessing would be dangerous. The urge to trace her fingertips along the edge of his gorgeous jawline until the hard muscles relaxed was difficult to fight. Twisting the ends of her scarf kept her hands distracted, but not much would help her heart. "Is that what you wanted to talk about?"

"Anjelica, I need to apologize."

"No. Please don't."

He turned his gaze to her. The green-gray of his eyes looked alive. "I broke what we had and I want to fix it." One step and he was close enough to kiss her.

Her heart slammed against its cage as if to reach out to him, wanting to touch him. She wasn't sure she could refuse him again.

"Yes. You're more than the nanny. There is something between us, but I'm so messed up I don't know how to handle this—" he waved his hand "—thing between us. I've never been in a normal relationship. I've never been with someone that didn't need me to save them."

He reached down and took her hand in his. "With my inappropriate proposal, I drove you away instead of making us closer." His other hand went to her chin. "Please let me fix it. I'm not sure how, but I want to fix what I broke."

Biting the inside of her cheek, she prayed. *Please don't let me cry.* "What do you want from me?"

"I want you to give us a chance to get to know each other as two adults. Would you go on a date with me? Just the two of us. I'll get a babysitter, maybe my mom."

She couldn't help but laugh. "I think we've gone about this the wrong way. First there were children, then you ask me to marry you. Now you're asking me on a date?"

"I told you I wasn't good at this relationship stuff. I was married to a woman that thought it was okay to date other people. I had a father that did the same to my mom. So this whole attempt at a normal relationship is new, and I might make some mistakes."

With the most earnest expression she'd ever seen, he took her other hand. She tried not to laugh, she really did. Biting down on her lip didn't hide it from him, though.

"Are you laughing at me?" His left eyebrow arched.

Shaking her head, she took a deep breath and gained some control. It would kill her to hurt his feelings, especially since he guarded them so well.

A lopsided grin pulled on the corner of his lips, causing her favorite dimple to make an appearance.

She caressed the sweet line on his cheek. Anticipation of a kiss started to burn.

Instead he moved back. "I concede."

Disappointment should not have been her reaction. Wanting kisses from him after turning down his proposal would just confuse them more.

His gaze searched her face. "Can I kiss you?"

Every muscle in her body tightened. If she didn't respond, would that be a yes? She stood still and waited.

"I'll take that as a yes." Those beautiful eyes of his closed as his lips made contact with hers.

Melting into him sounded like a good option.

Strong hands full of warmth cupped her jaw as he gently explored the corner of her mouth. He broke contact first, taking her scarf with him.

"Hey, that's mine." She reached for it.

With a quick move, he kissed the scar next to her ear. "You can get it back Thursday at seven when I pick you up for our date." Mischief danced as the green became intense in his eyes. "You're so beautiful you don't need it."

With one last grin, he turned and headed back to his mother and kids.

"I never said yes!" she yelled after him.

Waving her scarf like a flag won in combat, Garrett turned and had the gall to laugh. "Oh yes, you did. Sweetheart, I might have had my doubts earlier, but after that kiss? You said a whole lot, and yes to Thursday night was just the beginning." He continued to walk backward until he reached the corner of the house. Tossing his chin up, he winked, turned and disappeared behind the wall.

Hands crossed over her chest. Fingers wrapped around the thin straps of her sundress. The cool breeze brushed her exposed skin. She tried to remember the last time she'd been outside without one of her scarves.

Tears moistened her lashes and burned her eyes. It had been about the same time she lost the only person who knew her enough to know what her kiss meant.

Steve had teased her that they had been together so long they could read each other's minds.

All the way back to preschool, when he had publicly claimed her as his wife. The wedding ceremony had taken place in the house center. Her cousin Diego had married them. The baby dolls and stuffed animals had witnessed the whole event. Steve had worn a fireman's hat, and she'd worn the lace veil from the dress-up box.

Her fingers became numb as her nails cut into the

flesh of her palms. She'd never dreamed that kind of friendship—that kind of love—could be hers again.

Relaxing her fingers, she took a deep breath. Her house was just like the play center at the preschool. She went through the motions of pretending to have a life.

She had the nerve to tell Garrett he needed to open up and love the children up close.

She bowed her head and the tears fell hard. *God, forgive me for my self-righteous attitude. Thank You for opening my heart to see the truth of the walls I built to keep people out.*

Something brushed her leg. Opening her eyes, she found Selena sitting at her feet. The dog looked up with compassion in her blue and brown eyes.

Anjelica went to her knees and buried her face in the soft fur. "You're always taking care of the family, aren't you, girl?"

Anjelica's tears wet Selena's coat. Her sobs were soft as the tears released the truth of her own lies.

A wet nose pressed up against her neck. "Thank you, Selena." She stood. "Go watch over the family. I'll be back at dinnertime."

With one last pat to Selena, she moved to her car. God had given her a gift in Steve, and now it appeared she had gotten another. A whole family this time.

Was she brave enough to take a chance and love again?

Garrett stood at the nursery window. His stomach in a knot. He had made her cry. He thought of going out there. But afraid of making it worse, he hid inside behind the curtain like a coward. So the dog was a better person than he was.

He'd so missed the mark on that one. When he left

her, he'd felt better than he had in…well, forever. That perfect kiss, apparently not so perfect for her. What had he done wrong now?

Idiot, he had taken her scarf thinking it would show her how beautiful she was to him. Well, that backfired. He needed a manual. Maybe he could ask his mom, but she and Anjelica seemed so different.

"Garrett, is everything okay?" His mother stood beside him, looking out the window. "You seemed very happy after your talk with Anjelica. What's wrong now?"

"I think I messed up." Her old Ford truck vanished over the hill, out of his sight. Turning to his mother, he smiled. "I'm really glad you're here, Mom." He glanced around her shoulder. "Rio fell asleep?"

"Before I got to the third page." She laid her hand on his arm. "Now it's just the two of us. Let's talk."

They settled on the sofa with the box of memories between them. "You need to stop thanking me for being here. I should've dropped everything and been on your doorstep the minute you called me." She closed the lid and ran her hand over the top. "I should've loved you more than I resented Viviana. But tell me about Anjelica. Are you dating?"

He snorted. Tilting his head back on the sofa, he closed his eyes. "I actually asked her to marry me. She said no. So today I asked her on a date. Come to think of it, I didn't ask her. I told her I would pick her up Thursday at seven. I was trying to fix everything, but I think I might've made it worse."

He didn't know what he expected, but gut-busting laughter was not it. "Oh, sweetheart, you are so messed up." She leaned toward him. "Tell me, how did you propose?"

He groaned. "I told her marriage between us would be good for the kids because she loved them better than I could. Her home would be a good place to raise them. Then I followed up by telling her I couldn't love her the way she wanted."

"And she told you no? Shocking." She gave him a teasing wink.

"One thing you did well as a mom was make us laugh at ourselves. There wasn't any problem too big."

"Yeah, well, I would have never gotten out of bed if I let the problems keep me down. A good sense of humor and God will get you far, or at least keep you from crying all the time." She patted his arm. "And what is this about you not loving people enough? Where did that hogwash come from? That's not even true. You might pretend to be a big bad loner, but you're not. The very core of you is the faithful protector. You were made to be a father and husband. You're lying to yourself, and her, if you say you can't love completely."

"I'm starting to think that might be true."

"Believe me, I know the difference. So what are you going to do about it?"

"First I want to focus on the court date we have coming up. I need to make sure I get guardianship of Pilar. Then I'll figure out what to do with Anjelica. I need to get myself straightened out before I can offer her more." He would talk to Jake about seeing that therapist. "What about you, Mom? Who is this Hank person you've spoken of?" He used his deep manly voice, and it made her laugh. He had lived for her laughter when he was small. A mom's laughter made the world a better place.

"I actually met him at a singles' party at the new church I'm attending. He's one of the youth directors. His wife died a few years back. He has three grown children and a grandchild. He's encouraged me to stop hating and blaming your father by forgiving him, even though he didn't ask for it. Or even deserve it. I'm taking back my life. I'm taking back my happy. I'm not letting other people hold my heart hostage anymore." She cupped his face. "How can I hate a man that gave me two amazing children?"

"We get the amazing part from you."

"See, you always say the right thing. You need to be a husband to a woman that will love you back. Your Anjelica seems very solid and family oriented, and she would be blessed to have you."

He sighed. If it were only that easy. "You hungry? I can heat up some soup Anjelica made from scratch."

"She cooks, too! Are you sure she's human?"

He chuckled. "Sometimes I wonder." *Okay, God. I need a plan. Your plan. Show me the way.* Si Dios quiere.

Chapter Fourteen

Garrett tried to set Rio down next to the toy train. Their day in court had arrived, and their case had finally been called up. He smiled at Rio. "Come on, little man. I always wanted a train when I was a kid." He pushed it down the tracks and made train noises.

Rio wouldn't let go of his arm. "I want to stay with you."

"I need you to stay here with Pilar. Babies aren't allowed in the courtroom."

One of the women with a ruffled apron joined them. "Are you Rio? I'm Colleen. I'll be here with you and your sister until your daddy can come back. Pilar is playing with a truck. Do you want to join her?"

Large eyes full of a fear that twisted Garrett's gut looked up at him. "You're coming back? They're not going to take us away?"

"I promise. You're my son. They can't take you from me."

"Are they going to take Pilar?" With his face buried in Garrett's jacket, the words came out muffled.

What did he say without lying? "We're going to talk

to the judge. Pilar's grandmother wants to spend time with her, too."

Rio pulled back and looked at Garrett. "I can talk to the judge. You said I should use my words to get what I want." Tears formed in his eyes.

Pressing his lips to the top of the curly hair, Garrett glanced at Anjelica in desperation. Pilar was pushing a truck along as she crawled behind it.

The urge to grab them and not look back sounded good right about now. Now it was clear why some parents ran with their kids.

Colleen put her hands under Rio's arms and pulled him toward her. "Come on, Rio. The faster your dad goes, the faster he'll be back."

Garrett pulled his arm out of Rio's grasp. His son started crying. *God help me—I can't do this.*

A warm touch grounded him. He turned and found Anjelica.

"We'll be back, Rio." Her hand slid down to Garrett's and she intertwined her fingers with his. With a squeeze of his hand, she leaned in close to his ear. "Smile at him and walk out the door like you know you're coming back."

With a smile, he winked at Rio and did as she said. He stepped into the hallway with all the confidence that he'd be back to take his family home, his whole family.

Once they got past the door, he leaned against the wall to slow his pulse and gain some form of control over his emotions. He had to appear calm and confident going into the courtroom, even if he needed to fake it.

Anjelica stopped next to him. "That was hard, but the longer you stood there, the more uncertain he would have become."

He sighed. "I know. The fear of disappointing him

took over." A halfhearted grin pulled at his mouth. "For a moment, I thought I could grab them and run. What am I going to do if the judge gives Pilar to the grand-mother?"

"We'll fight it. You can also make sure Rio gets to visit with her. But I just know you'll get her. I can't imagine the judge separating them."

He nodded. Sometimes he wished he had her optimism, but he knew the realities of life. Life was not fair, and the good guy didn't always win.

He wasn't even the good guy. "Thank you for being here. I meant to bring your scarf to you today. I shouldn't have taken it from you."

Her delicate shoulders shrugged and a sweet look of understanding he didn't deserve settled on her face. "If I wanted it back, I could have gotten it. I know where you live. I'll get it from you Thursday when you pick me up. Where are we going?"

"Are you sure you want to go out with me? I didn't really ask you and…" He didn't want her to know he had seen her cry afterward. "I didn't really ask."

"Oh, if you changed your mind—"

"No, I still want to go with you if you want to go. There's a place on the river in Kerrville that plays live jazz on their patio Thursday nights."

"Sounds lovely."

"Okay. Good."

His mother walked down the corridor. "Sharon said they're ready." She gave him a tentative smile. With her hair up, she looked too young to be his mother. Taking his hand, she gave him a reassuring smile. "Do you want to have a quick prayer before we go?"

He nodded. Anjelica moved in closer and took his other hand.

He opened his heart to God's will as he regulated his breathing. "Lord, please cover the courtroom with Your presence. Wrap Rio and Pilar so tightly in Your love that they'll always know You. Grant wisdom on the judge, and give me peace for Your will."

Both women squeezed his hands. He leaned over and kissed his mother on the cheek. "Thank you for being here."

"I should have been here sooner."

"You're here now. Come on—let's get this settled and hopefully have everyone home in time for dinner."

Walking into the courtroom, he stopped at the sight that greeted him. In the benches were Anjelica's parents, a few sisters and her grandparents. That didn't surprise him as much as the other couples who now stood to greet him. The sheriff, Jake Torres, and his wife, Vickie, were with Pastor John and his fiancée, Anjelica's cousin Lorrie Ann. Maggie and Yolanda, along with a few other Ortegas, filled the room. A couple of people from the church joined the group as they surrounded him.

His chest burned as if someone had punched him. They were here to support him. To help him keep his family together.

He tried swallowing, but his throat was too dry. He thought about something as they each shook his hand and encouraged him. He knew the community was tight and supportive, but somehow he'd missed the memo that he was a member of the community himself. This wasn't just for Anjelica; they were here for him, Rio and Pilar.

Smiling, he nodded and patted each handshake with his left hand on top of his right. Anjelica hugged people, tears sitting softly on her eyelashes. Instead of making her look weak, they showed how strong she was.

Anjelica had the sense to introduce his mother to everyone. Looking over, he saw Cecilia Barrow, Pilar's grandmother, sitting with a teenage girl. He thought it could be one of the granddaughters she was raising, but he wasn't sure.

The CPS caseworker was talking to her. No matter how many deep breaths he took, the knot in his stomach pulled tighter.

The judge entered the room and everyone got in place. After calling the court to order, she asked the child advocacy and CPS workers to approach the bench.

Everyone took a seat and waited for the judge's decision. She scanned the larger audience behind Garrett and Anjelica.

She looked down at her paper. "For me, when family comes into court wanting to keep a grandchild, it is an easy decision when that grandparent has a good record and has shown commitment to other grandchildren she has taken custody of. This has a little bit of a complication because the child in question also has a brother that has a father. Overall, I do believe blood relations are the best place for a child to feel like they belong."

Garrett was going to be sick. He wanted to stand and yell no.

Pilar's grandmother stood. "I'm sorry to interrupt, Your Honor, but is there a way I may speak to Mr. Kincaid alone before going any further?"

The judge raised an eyebrow. "I will let you ask him here. I would prefer to do this quickly. Will you and Mr. Kincaid please approach the bench?"

Reaching for Anjelica's hand, he looked back in

surprise when she didn't follow. She shook her head, and he let her go. He wanted her by his side, but she didn't have legal rights to be there. There were a few times in his life he'd been this scared, and they had always ended in disaster.

He glanced at Cecilia before turning to the judge. With no clue what she was up to, he couldn't even begin to sort his emotions.

"What did you want to ask Officer Kincaid?"

The older woman who was already raising her other grandchildren looked up at him. Her dark hair streaked with silver was pulled into a tight neat bun. "I was just told you had already had a lawyer put the money for both children into a trust fund you can't touch. Is that correct?"

That took him by surprise. Whatever he'd thought she might want to know, that was not it. Was she mad she couldn't get to the money?

"Yes. It can be used for college at any time, but if they don't go to college, then they'll get their portion when they're twenty-five. Do you have a problem with that? I worked it out with the CPS workers and the lawyers."

The wrinkles at the corners of her eyes elongated with her smile. "No, the reason I stepped in and filed for custody of baby Pilar was to protect her from being used for any money she might get."

"I don't need the money, and truthfully, I wouldn't want it either way."

She nodded and turned back to the judge. "I'm sorry, but I would like to withdraw my claim of custody to Pilar. I would like visitations but not guardianship."

"This hearing was for guardianship." Impatience

clipped the judge's words. "You can work out visitation between the two of you."

Stunned, Garrett was afraid of falling. His legs had disappeared from under him. She had withdrawn her claim. Pilar was his, for now.

"Yes!" He blinked back the burn in his eyes. "Yes, you can visit Pilar." He turned. Anjelica stood.

Even across the room, she helped him keep his feet in place. The judge might frown on him running from the room to get his children. His children. He bit down hard on the inside of his cheek. He had to keep it under control. There were still a few months before he could adopt her.

Dismissed by the judge, he went straight to Anjelica. He felt light as a helium balloon, and Anjelica's hand was the string that kept him earthbound.

With her hand in his, he faced all the people who had come to support him. Everyone had questions in their eyes. They hadn't heard the exchange from the front of the court. He smiled the first real smile all day.

"She dropped the claim. Pilar's mine. We're taking her home." Cheers erupted. Hugs and pats on the back made him feel like a new father who had just been told his baby had arrived healthy in the hospital. Standing to the side was his mother. Tears ran down her cheeks. Leaving the boisterous crowd, he went to her.

"We won."

With a napkin, she wiped under her eyes. "I'm so proud of you, Garrett. And I think, as a mother, Viviana is very happy about this outcome."

"I hope so. Come on—I want to tell Rio."

With his arm around his mother's slender waist, they

went through the sea of people and to the door. Cecilia stood there.

"You have a lot of friends and family that are happy for you. That's good to see. I just wanted to make sure you were serious about me being able to visit her."

"I never meant to keep her away from you. You're more than welcome to visit. Do you want to see her now?"

Dark eyes lit up. "Can I? Thank you."

"Hello, I'm Garrett's mother. I just want you to know, from one grandmother to another, that Pilar is well loved. Thank you for letting him keep the children together."

The older woman looked over to the bench where her other granddaughter sat staring at a phone with earbuds blocking out the world. "I'm getting too old to raise kids." She looked through the window where the children played. "He wasn't always bad. Drugs eat the core of a person and gut them, taking control. I thought with Viviana and Pilar things were getting better. I prayed so hard. Then he lost his job. He cut me off, not allowing me to come over or see the kids. I feared he had gotten back into that world."

She turned her head and wiped at the tears. "Sorry. I just never dreamed it would end like this. At one time, he was a good boy. I want Pilar to know that about her father."

Garrett put a hand on her shoulder. "You can share the good parts with her. As they get older, there will be a lot of tough questions to answer. I'm glad you want to stay in her life. I think that'll help them sort through it. Let's go see them."

His mother, Pilar's grandmother and Anjelica joined him as he crossed the threshold to his children.

Rio stood when they walked into the playroom. Panic screamed from his eyes as he stood in front of his sister. Going to one knee in front of his son, Garrett laid a hand on one small shoulder. Rio's back was stiff as he glared at Pilar's grandmother. The little guy was ready to fight for his sister.

"Relax. She just came in to see Pilar. The judge agreed that the best place for you and Pilar to live was with me."

The eyes that looked so much like his own darted to him. "And Anjelica?"

"She'll still be in the big house." The only thing left now was to settle the role she played in their lives.

"Hello, Rio. Do you remember me? I'm Grandma CeCe."

"Grandmas are good to have, right?" He glanced over at Anjelica and Garrett's mother.

Anjelica joined him on the floor. "Oh yes. The more grandmothers, the better."

After a nod from Rio, Cecilia moved around to Pilar. "Oh, sweet girl."

While Cecilia talked to Pilar, Garrett pulled Rio into his arms. He wanted to absorb the scent and feel of his son. The day could have been devastating, but it wasn't. He was now one step closer to officially being their father. They were his children.

Not that long ago, he thought his plan in life was to build a cabin and live alone. Jake had made a joke about plans that he now understood.

A greater life waited for him, one he hadn't even known he wanted. Eyes closed, he pressed his lips against the soft curly hair of his son.

When he lifted his head, Anjelica was there, tears

in her eyes and joy on her face. "You did it. They're coming home."

"I'm so ready to get out of here. We need to celebrate."

Colleen brought the diaper bag to them. "Congratulations. Some families are just meant to be together."

"Rio, go with Anjelica. I'll get your sister."

After one last kiss from Grandma CeCe, Garrett took Pilar. The urge to squeeze her riveted his muscles. Taking a deep breath, he relaxed his arms. The baby shampoo Anjelica had bought for her smelled of comfort and love. She was his. Oh man. If he didn't get a grip, he'd be crying in front of people.

His mother held out a cup of coffee. "Here, I know you didn't want any before the hearing, but you deserve it now."

"Thanks."

Diaper bag over his shoulder, his daughter in one arm and coffee in his hand, he followed Anjelica out of the courthouse. A new adventure waited. Now if he could just convince Anjelica to join him, life would be perfect.

A flash of heat rushed his body. A cold sweat covered his skin. Taking a sip of coffee, he mentally grounded himself. Just because life was good didn't mean something bad was about to happen.

Pilar touched his face with her now-chubby fingers. "Dada."

Anjelica gasped. "Did she just call you Dada?"

His mother clapped. "She did. Are these her first words?" She pulled her phone out. "Dada. See if you can get her to say it again."

"Mom, really?"

"Oh, don't play Mr. Tough Guy. We know you better and I saw you almost tear up. This is big. You will thank me for recording it. She'll be grown up and having her own family before you know what's happening."

"Mom. She's not even a year yet."

Pilar patted his face to get his attention. "Dada. Dada."

Ugh. His mom was right—he wanted to cry. He hated emotion. "I'm right here, baby girl."

"I can say *Daddy*, too. I'm a big boy, so I know how to say it right."

Standing at the car door, Garrett laughed. "Yes, and it takes time to learn how to say words. I remember someone not using his words not that long ago."

Anjelica opened the door and got Rio in his car seat. "Yep, words have power. We're proud of both of you."

"Dada! Dada!" Pilar giggled. "Dada! Dada!" She smiled as everyone told her how smart she was. "Dada!"

His heart officially belonged to her. No one had ever told him how a single word would change his life.

"I think this deserves ice cream. My treat." His mom climbed into the backseat between the car seats.

He couldn't help but smile. "Some of my favorite memories were you taking us to get ice cream when we had good grades or you got a new job."

"I wish I could have done more."

He gave his mom the best father look he could manage. He'd have to practice. "You raised some pretty good kids, Mom."

"Yes, I did."

Closing the door, he pressed all of his weight into his hands. Leaning hard against the car. The smell of rain hung in the air. Fresh and clean, washing away the dust. He had a new plan. Now, how to go about making it happen without messing everything up?

Getting in the car, he was greeted with "Dada! Dada!"

Everyone laughed as Pilar gave him a huge grin, kicking her feet. "Dada! Dada!"

Anjelica winked at him. "I think we might have created a monster."

"She's our monster now."

Chapter Fifteen

Three weeks had passed since the first date with Anjelica. He'd managed to get one more date in and several family excursions.

Garrett heaved a huge sigh of relief in the empty room. All the family noise outside was muffled. The church had been standing-room only for the Easter service, and now it seemed as if everyone had followed them home.

His guess? They picked up a few strays along the way. Anjelica had even invited Cecilia for the festivities, and Pilar's grandmother brought three of her older grandkids.

When he planned for a family Easter-egg hunt and dinner, he had foolishly imagined her parents and his kids. Maybe a few aunts and uncles and her favorite cousins. A perfect time to propose. But now it was a whole town event.

He hadn't been near this nervous when he asked Viviana to marry him. Then again, he had been naive and full of the fantasy of marriage.

Harsh reality replaced fantasies. The pendulum swung back. He'd gone from thinking marriage would fix him, to thinking marriage was a death trap, to thinking marriage would fix his children. Now he settled somewhere in the middle.

Taking the ring out of his pocket, he wondered if it was too soon. He was ready to completely commit, but would she believe him?

She had turned him down once for every right reason. His hand shook a little when he placed the ring on the shelf above Steve's flag and picture.

"Well, I'm gonna try and get it right this time. Any suggestions? You loved the girl she was, and I hope she lets me love the woman she's become." Could he compete with a childhood love?

"Garrett?"

He jumped at the sound of his mother's voice.

"Who are you talking to?"

"Is it weird that I'm talking to her husband?"

She came over and rested her cheek on his upper arm as she looked up at the pictures. "No. You're both marines. You've seen the same things, loved the same girl. You have a great deal in common." She reached up and kissed him on the cheek. "Oh, Garrett! Is that box what I think it is?"

He nodded. "Somewhere in my addled brain, I thought today would be a great time to ask her. A grand romantic gesture in front of her family. I planned to hide it in an Easter egg with her name on it. Now it sounds lame. What if one of the kids finds it?" He went to the window and peeked through the curtains. The front was packed with cars and trucks. "I also don't want her to feel trapped. If I ask her in front of everyone…well, that might not end up well."

He put his left arm around his mother as he ran his other hand through his hair. "I want to make it special.

Let her know how important she is to me. I don't know if this is good enough." He looked back at the picture. All the memories she must have made with Steve were everywhere. In the house, in town, at the church. How did he even begin to find a place in her life?

"Are you worried you haven't dated long enough?"

He snorted. "That's one concern that never occurred to me. I know her. We've shared as many breakfasts, lunches and dinners as a married couple. When you pace the floor at three in the morning soothing a sick child together, you know that person in a deeper way than if you'd met for a year's worth of dates. I know her. But what if she knows me too well? What if I'm not enough for her to get over her fear of how I make a living?"

"Oh, sweetheart, you're more than enough."

"You're my mom. Your opinion doesn't count."

"You do what you feel is right, but promise me you won't let fear be the thing that stops you." She patted his chest. "Don't hide in here for too long, or Buela will come looking for you. The kids are about to hit the pi-ñata. Anjelica sent me in to get more tea. She said it was on the stove."

"I'll help you. Last thing I want is Buela hunting me down."

They took the fresh-brewed tea to the beverage table, and his mom helped him pour it into a giant orange dispenser. Scanning the backyard, he found Anjelica bouncing Pilar on her hip while she talked to Vickie, the sheriff's wife.

Her one free hand was waving about as she explained something. Her shoulders were bare except for the straps of the sundress she wore. He liked to think he had helped her feel more confident in some way.

Kids ran around. People talked and laughed. Someone was playing a guitar. A few of the men were stringing up a colorful star piñata, with the ribbon getting tangled in the wind. This was home.

His eyes went back to Anjelica. She was home.

A bump to the shoulder took him out of his own thoughts. Sheriff Torres stood there with a plateful of desserts. "You know you can go talk to her. You don't have to stare at her like a lovesick boy at a middle-school dance." He popped a lemon square in his mouth.

Garrett snorted. "I thought you already had dessert."

With a shrug, he glanced over to his wife and Anjelica. "Have to try everything to make sure no one's feelings get hurt. It's a sacrifice, but someone has to make sure it's done." He swung his gaze back to Garrett. "Speaking of sacrifice. How's family life treating you?"

Garrett found Rio running with several children. He laughed as a little mop of a dog jumped after him. Looked like Coach Valdez and his son had been invited, too. "Better than I thought."

"Yeah, it can take some getting used to. Still having good and bad days with Vickie's kids living with me." He laughed. "Vickie assures me it's normal. I wouldn't trade it for the world, though. Have you been seeing Reeves like I suggested?"

Nodding, Garrett kept an eye on Rio as the children ran behind the garden and around the Esperanza bush.

"Actually, it's helped a great deal. Thank you. I feel more grounded than I have since getting back to the States."

"Yeah, he's a good guy. Let me know if you need anything. I'm always available. I'm a good wingman, too. Just sayin'. Don't wait too long. I wasted ten years afraid to just ask." With a smirk on his face, his gaze darted from Anjelica back to Garrett. Vickie waved at them. "Duty calls. Catch you later."

"Later."

Vickie's daughter ran to Torres and jumped into his arms. Holding the girl, he spoke with the women for a while before taking off on a mission to hang the donkey piñata for the smaller kids.

He could stand here all day and watch Anjelica in action. She brought order to chaos and made it seem easy. Glancing over her shoulder, she caught him staring at her.

Great, he did look like that awkward middle-school kid. With a nod, he turned to take the large pot back to the kitchen.

Today was not the right time. He needed to wait, but the question was when. Rushing something this big was not good. He'd done that with Viviana. But waiting too long could waste time, like Torres said.

What if she found someone else who didn't carry a gun for a living? Like the coach. With a grunt, he opened the screen door.

Maybe it was a test. If he really loved her, he'd give up law enforcement. He washed the pot and put it away, then stood in the middle of the kitchen.

He couldn't imagine doing anything else. Rubbing his temple, he took a deep breath. This was too complicated. What was wrong with wanting a simple life? Then again, if he had stayed away from Viviana when he returned home, he wouldn't have Rio or Pilar. Now he was talking himself in circles. How could you regret a life that also brought you blessings?

Looking into the living room, he saw the ring on the high shelf. He needed to put it away for now.

* * *

Anjelica nodded at something Vickie said, but her attention stayed on the back door. Garrett hadn't smiled back at her when she caught him staring.

The last two days, he seemed distracted. She bit down on the inside of her cheek. What was wrong, and why was he not talking to her?

"Then a lion jumped from the stage and bit his head off."

She turned back to Vickie and blinked a couple of times. "What?"

"Oh, that you heard. So where did you go while Pilar and I had a talk?" She smiled at the little girl and tickled her tummy.

Pilar giggled and grabbed Anjelica's hair and pulled her close, slobbering on her cheek. "Oh, Anjelica. She's giving you kisses! She looks at you like you're her mamma."

Anjelica hugged her close. "Oh, baby girl, I love you, too." She glanced back at Vickie. "Enough of this mamma talk."

"Oh, give me a break. You take care of her. You practically live in the same house. You are basically her mamma. The only one she has or knows. The way her daddy has been looking at you, I say he wouldn't mind her calling you Mamma."

"We're just friends."

Vickie's eyebrow went high. "Is that what the kids are calling it these days? I thought you had gone on some real dates."

Shaking her head, she cupped Pilar's sweet face and kissed her dark curls. "We have, but I just don't think I can go down that road again."

"What road is that? Love? I think it might be too late."

Anjelica shook her head. "I married one man who had a hero complex. I can't sit at home and wait, praying he comes home." She looked at Vickie. "How do you not go crazy every time Jake goes to work?"

"First I pray every day to keep him protected." Vickie tilted her head. "But I don't get why you compare Steve to Garrett. I remember Steve pushing the edge all the time. He would rush headlong without thinking. Remember the time he jumped from one truck to another while they were going, like, eighty miles an hour? How many cars did he total?" She rolled her eyes. "That boy was downright crazy. I always thought you were the only reason he didn't get himself killed early on."

Anjelica blinked to keep tears from falling. Vickie laid a hand on her upper arm.

"I'm sorry. My mouth gets me in trouble all the time. I didn't mean to upset you. That was just stupid of me."

"No. I'm okay. I never really thought about it like that before. I loved Steve, but I spent a great deal of time waiting for him to grow up."

"He was a great kid. Biggest heart in the world, and he loved you. He also liked playing the hero, but not the way Jake and Garrett do. Garrett is smart. Jake's impressed with him. He considers the situation and takes charge. If that's the reason you're not sure, girl, you need to let that go." She looked back to the porch. "You have a great man there, and if I'm reading it right, he's in love with you."

"I don't know. The last few days he's been acting weird."

Vickie snorted. "Yeah! You're giving the poor guy every mixed message there is. Poor boys. We drive them crazy, but between you and me. I think they kinda like it." She reached for Pilar. "Let me take this little bit, and you go talk to your man. You're not wearing your scarves anymore—I'm guessing that has something to do with him. Put all the worries in God's hands and go."

Garrett was still in the house. She scanned the yard full of family and friends and realized he was alone inside. Maybe this was too much for him.

She was used to all the people all the time, but he was so private.

"Go. Stop overthinking it and go." Vickie waved her on.

"Okay, okay."

With a deep breath, her shoulders back, she walked forward. Why was she so nervous? Silence met her in the kitchen. "Garrett?"

"Anjelica? Do you need something?" His deep voice came from the living room.

They met at the archway as she moved into the living room and he walked into the kitchen.

He braced his hands on her arms so as not to run her over. "Everyone okay?"

"Yes. I just thought we could talk."

His eyebrows crunched down. "Now? Don't you have a few hundred guests outside?"

She bumped her fist against his upper arm. An upper arm that looked really good in the short-sleeved polo he wore. With a sigh, she looked up at his face. "Not that many. Is it making you nervous? I can ask them to leave. We've already done the Easter-egg hunt, and everyone's eaten."

With a grin on those perfect lips, he stepped back. Well, she couldn't trust herself to look at his face, either, without getting distracted. She'd always had a thing for jaws. Strong jaws and dimples. Like the long dimple on the side of… Ugh. *Focus, Anjelica.*

Now he had one eyebrow cocked, waiting for her to speak. Vickie was right. Garrett never rushed anything. Well, other than marriage. He'd rushed it with Viviana and tried with her.

Stepping into him, she cupped his face with her hands. Confusion clouded his expression. New stubble edged his jaw. His eyes searched her face.

Lifting her face, she pressed her lips to his. He closed his eyes. The muscles under her hand relaxed. Slowly, he joined the kiss, following her lead. She moved closer, wanting to sink into him and take him all in, his textures, his scent.

Fingers slid from his jaw to the pulse at the base of his neck.

Placing his hands on the backs of her arms, he pulled back. "Wow."

She was officially out of her mind. He had to think she was crazy. He was waiting for her to say something, but her brain knocked around her skull without a single idea. "Hi."

Really? That was all she had.

His lips moved to a wide-open smile. "Hi to you, too."

"I've really enjoyed these last three weeks with the kids."

"And the kids enjoy being with you."

She wrapped her arms around her middle and looked to the backyard. She'd never worried about her words with Steve.

Garrett looked relaxed with his hands in the front pockets of his jeans. An encouraging smile didn't really help her feel better.

"You know Steve was the only boy I ever dated, and we knew each other from the time we could walk. So this whole relationship thing is new to me, too."

"Ha. A normal relationship with a well-adjusted, strong woman is completely new territory for me. I…" He glanced over his shoulder into the living room. Coming back to her, he ran his hand through his hair, causing it to stand up on the side.

Not able to resist, she moved toward him and smoothed out the strays. "What is it?"

"Nothing. So you left the party to hunt me down and kiss me?"

She had to laugh. "You make me sound so…forward. The kiss was unexpected, but I hope it got the message across." Hand flat on his chest, she felt his heart beat. It seemed to pick up the pace. "I want to spend more time with you. Not because of the kids, but because I love you." There, she'd said it, and the house didn't fall down. Garrett was still standing, too. His face scrunched in a frown.

Okay, not the reaction she'd hoped for.

She looked for a way out. How did you make a graceful exit after saying those words? In one long step, he had his hands on her shoulders, anchoring her in place. No escaping now.

"You weren't supposed to say it first."

"What? It's a contest?"

He chuckled. "No. I've been debating for a week now, but worried I'd say it too soon. I really messed up last time, and I need to get this right.

"Last time? You've never said—" She covered her mouth when she realized he was talking about his marriage proposal. "The proposal? That was you saying you loved me?"

"Not very well." Holding his palm up, he waited for her to take his offer. "Come with me. I want to show you something."

They joined hands, and his thumb caressed the back of her hand. So much bigger than hers, his fingers engulfed her hand, making her feel safe and cherished.

She followed him out the kitchen door and up the stairs to his apartment. Now she was curious. What could be in the apartment she had not seen before?

In his living room, he dropped her hand. "Wait here." He disappeared into his room. Nerves started twisting as she tried to imagine what he wanted to show her.

Joining her, he held a boot box. Okay, so it wasn't a ring. Balancing the box with one hand, he lifted the lid. He pulled out a string? He stopped and looked at her. Uncertainty suddenly appeared on his face.

"What is it? You're killing me."

"I know we both have broken pieces, but I hope together we can make a family. I love you and can't imagine anyone else. I don't want anyone else."

With a lopsided grin, he lowered the box. Hanging from the string was her broken wind chime that had been destroyed in the storm.

Her hand covered her mouth. The one she had made when she was expecting Esperanza. She thought she'd lost it forever. Now he offered it back to her.

It was cracked and skewed, but he had glued the parts together. A few were missing, but it was beautiful. She wanted to cry.

Carefully, he put it back in the box. "I'm sorry. I didn't mean—"

Just like Rio, she launched herself at him. His arms came around her as he staggered back. His laughter rumbled from his chest.

"So you like it?"

"It's the nicest, best gift anyone has ever given me." Giving him some space, she stepped back and wiped her face.

"I had a whole speech to go with it. I know this might be too soon, but we've been through so much and I can't imagine more time will change anything for me." He took a knee in front of her and pulled a small box out of his pocket. "I know I'm not the easiest man to get along with, but I want to be there for you. You know me in ways no one else ever even tried to know me." He took a solitaire out of its velvet box. "Anjelica Ortega-Garza, will you accept all my broken parts and add Kincaid to your name?"

"Are you willing to take on the Ortega family and all that means?"

His dimples came out in full force. "Yes. I almost love them as much as I love you."

"Then yes! Garrett River Kincaid, I would be proud to marry you and be your wife."

Somehow his grin grew wider and he slipped the ring on her finger. It was a touch too big. His smile disappeared. "We'll have to get it sized, or you can pick another one."

Holding her hand up, she admired the swirl and twist of the gold band surrounding the simple classic diamond. "It's perfect." She took a deep breath and wrapped her arms around his neck. "I love you."

He glanced at the door. "We should go tell Rio and your family."

She let go of his neck and took his hand. She just wanted to stay there and absorb this moment with him. The love and happiness so complete it made her aware how empty she'd been before, going through the motions of living.

"Thank you, Garrett. For not giving up on me. I was so afraid of taking back my own happiness."

Cupping her face, he leaned in and kissed her. "Thank you."

With a nod, she turned to the door to make the announcement that would send her life in a new direction. A direction filled with love and laughter, even during the rough times.

Anjelica's hand in his, Garrett wanted to jump down the steps. Colorful confetti coated the yard. The *cascarones* wars must have broken out.

Many of the people turned and stared at them. Garrett was sure he had an expression on his face that gave them away. He scanned the yard for Rio.

From a group of children, his son ran toward him with one hand tucked behind his back. "Daddy, I have a secret."

Garrett leaned down, and Rio broke the confetti egg over his head. The boy laughed out loud, arching his whole body backward. "I got you, Daddy!"

"You did." Garrett shook his head and the colored paper flew around them.

"I have a secret, too. You wanna know what I did today?"

Rio looked at his hands with suspicion before getting closer. "What is it?"

He held out his hand to Anjelica. "I asked Anjelica to be my wife and your mother."

The little boy's eyes went wider as his gaze darted to Anjelica. He pressed his body against Garrett's side. "What did she say?" He whispered it, but the crowd had gotten quiet and it carried across the yard. It seemed as if the whole town waited for the answer.

Anjelica came down to Rio's eye level. "I said yes. Once we get married, we'll all live here together."

He whooped loud and jumped up. Before Garrett knew what had happened, they were surrounded. He picked Rio up so the crowd wouldn't overwhelm him.

This was his family. Every single person here was now a part of his future. He thought about the cabin he had planned. And didn't feel a twinge of regret or longing about it.

As people gathered and congratulated them, he kept his attention on Anjelica. Someone handed Pilar to her. They were so beautiful.

Parts of him might be forever broken, but the best parts now belonged to her. God really did answer prayers not even prayed for. He'd sent Garrett his very own hero, and now she was going to be his wife. He wanted to laugh and dance. God was good. Life was good. Love was his.

* * * * *

Dear Reader,

Thank you for joining me in Clear Water, Texas. It's one of my favorite places. Garrett has been in my thoughts for a few years. When Anjelica showed up in *Lone Star Hero* and walked away from Jake because she couldn't deal with a man in law enforcement, I knew I had found the perfect love for my wounded hero.

Thanks to my cousin Baron Von Guinther, I got to know Garrett better. Sitting by the bay in San Diego, we spent hours talking about marines and some of the things that make them tick. I fell in love with Garrett and watching the healing that a hurt little boy, a baby girl and a strong heroine could bring to his life. They all learned that no wound is too big for God.

I would also like to thank my cousins Chad Van Pelt and Forrest French along with their families for their service.

I love talking with readers. You can find me on Facebook at Jolene Navarro, Author, or visit my boards on Pinterest at Jolene Navarro.

Blessings,
Jolene Navarro

COMING NEXT MONTH FROM
Love Inspired®

Available September 20, 2016

THE RANCHER'S TEXAS MATCH
Lone Star Cowboy League: Boys Ranch
by Brenda Minton
Rancher Tanner Barstow knows Macy Swanson is only in Haven, Texas, to claim guardianship of her nephew. But can he convince the city girl to give small-town life—and him—a chance?

LONE STAR DAD
The Buchanons • by Linda Goodnight
Gena Satterfield is surprised when her solitary neighbor Quinn Buchanon starts bonding with her rebellious nephew. He's got a way with the boy—and with her heart—but the secret she's hiding may just tear them apart forever.

LOVING ISAAC
Lancaster County Weddings • by Rebecca Kertz
Isaac Lapp is looking to make amends for the mistakes of his past. Having once abandoned her for the *Englisch* life, can he convince his long-ago friend Ellen Mast of his promise...and of his love?

HOMETOWN HOLIDAY REUNION
Oaks Crossing • by Mia Ross
In town to temporarily run the family business, Cam Stewart begins to reconsider his stay when he reconnects with Erin Kinsley. His best friend's little sister has grown into a lovely woman—one he hopes to make a part of his permanent family.

A TEMPORARY COURTSHIP
Maple Springs • by Jenna Mindel
A chance at a coveted promotion has Darren Zelinsky teaching a class in Bay Willows, where he instantly becomes smitten with Bree Anderson. The charming musician will soon be heading west, unless the hometown boy can show her that her future lies with him.

A FAMILY FOR THE FARMER
by Laurel Blount
Farmer Abel Whitlock is determined to help single mom Emily Elliot run Goosefeather Farm. If she fails, he'll inherit. But he has no interest in claiming the land—he's after claiming his longtime crush's heart.

LOOK FOR THESE AND OTHER LOVE INSPIRED BOOKS WHEREVER BOOKS ARE SOLD, INCLUDING MOST BOOKSTORES, SUPERMARKETS, DISCOUNT STORES AND DRUGSTORES.

LICNM0916

REQUEST YOUR FREE BOOKS!

2 FREE INSPIRATIONAL NOVELS

PLUS 2
FREE
MYSTERY GIFTS

Love Inspired®

YES! Please send me 2 FREE Love Inspired® novels and my 2 FREE mystery gifts (gifts are worth about $10). After receiving them, if I don't wish to receive any more books, I can return the shipping statement marked "cancel." If I don't cancel, I will receive 6 brand-new novels every month and be billed just $4.99 per book in the U.S. or $5.49 per book in Canada. That's a saving of at least 17% off the cover price. It's quite a bargain! Shipping and handling is just 50¢ per book in the U.S. and 75¢ per book in Canada.* I understand that accepting the 2 free books and gifts places me under no obligation to buy anything. I can always return a shipment and cancel at any time. Even if I never buy another book, the two free books and gifts are mine to keep forever.   105/305 IDN GH5P

Name _____ (PLEASE PRINT) _____

Address _____ Apt. #

City _____ State/Prov. _____ Zip/Postal Code

Signature (if under 18, a parent or guardian must sign)

Mail to the **Reader Service:**
IN U.S.A.: P.O. Box 1867, Buffalo, NY 14240-1867
IN CANADA: P.O. Box 609, Fort Erie, Ontario L2A 5X3

Are you a subscriber to Love Inspired® books
and want to receive the larger-print edition?
Call 1-800-873-8635 or visit www.ReaderService.com.

* Terms and prices subject to change without notice. Prices do not include applicable taxes. Sales tax applicable in N.Y. Canadian residents will be charged applicable taxes. Offer not valid in Quebec. This offer is limited to one order per household. Not valid for current subscribers to Love Inspired books. All orders subject to credit approval. Credit or debit balances in a customer's account(s) may be offset by any other outstanding balance owed by or to the customer. Please allow 4 to 6 weeks for delivery. Offer available while quantities last.

Your Privacy—The Reader Service is committed to protecting your privacy. Our Privacy Policy is available online at www.ReaderService.com or upon request from the Reader Service.

We make a portion of our mailing list available to reputable third parties that offer products we believe may interest you. If you prefer that we not exchange your name with third parties, or if you wish to clarify or modify your communication preferences, please visit us at www.ReaderService.com/consumerschoice or write to us at Reader Service Preference Service, P.O. Box 9062, Buffalo, NY 14240-9062. Include your complete name and address.

LI15

*When Macy Swanson must suddenly raise her young
nephew, help comes in the form of single rancher and
boys ranch volunteer Tanner Barstow. Can he help her
see she's mom—and rural Texas—material?*

Read on for a sneak preview of the first book in the
LONE STAR COWBOY LEAGUE: BOYS RANCH
miniseries, THE RANCHER'S TEXAS MATCH
by Brenda Minton.

She leaned back in the seat and covered her face with her
hands. "I am angry. I'm mad because I don't know what to
do for Colby. And the person I always went to for advice
is gone. Grant is gone. I think Colby and I were both in
a delusional state, thinking they would come home. But
they're not. I'm not getting my brother, my best friend,
back. Colby isn't getting his parents back. And it isn't
fair. It isn't fair that I had to—"

Her eyes closed, and she shook her head.

"Macy?"

She pinched the bridge of her nose. "No. I'm not going
to say that. I lost a job and gave up an apartment. Colby
lost his parents. What I lost doesn't amount to anything. I
lost things I don't miss."

"I think you're wrong. I think you miss your life.
There's nothing wrong with that. Accept it, or it'll eat
you up."

Tanner pulled up to her house.

"I miss my life." She said it on a sigh. "I wouldn't be anywhere else. But I have to admit, there are days I wonder if Colby would be better off with someone else, with anyone but me. But I'm his family. We have each other."

"Yes, and in the end, that matters."

"But…" She bit down on her lip and glanced away from him, not finishing.

"But what?"

"What if I'm not a mom? What if I can't do this?" She looked young sitting next to him, her green eyes troubled.

"I'm guessing that even a mom who planned on having a child would still question if she could do it."

She reached for the door. "Thank you for letting me talk about Colby."

"Anytime." He said it, and then he realized the door that had opened.

She laughed. "Don't worry. I won't be calling at midnight to talk about my feelings."

"If you did, I'd answer."

She stood on tiptoe and touched his cheek to bring it down to her level. When she kissed him, he felt floored by the unexpected gesture. Macy had soft hair, soft gestures and a soft heart. She was easy to like. He guessed if a man wasn't careful, he'd find himself falling a little in love with her.

Don't miss
THE RANCHER'S TEXAS MATCH by Brenda Minton,
available October 2016 wherever
Love Inspired® books and ebooks are sold.

www.LoveInspired.com

Love the Love Inspired book you just read?

Your opinion matters.

Review this book on your favorite book site, review site, blog or your own social media properties and share your opinion with other readers!